Born and raised in County Durham in the Northeast of England, Karen emigrated to New Zealand at 16 and went to school and university there, before taking a job teaching History and English in a remote school in Central Otago. Karen returned to England to study for a Master's degree at Newcastle University. She taught in comprehensive schools in the Northeast until she took early retirement to travel with her husband and to lecture on cruise ships. She has one daughter, Katy, and a grandson, Jack.

For Trevor, Katy, David, and Jack.

Karen Cartmell

A VANISHED HAND

AUSTIN MACAULEY PUBLISHERS™
LONDON • CAMBRIDGE • NEW YORK • SHARJAH

Copyright © Karen Cartmell 2022

The right of Karen Cartmell to be identified as author of this work has been asserted by the author in accordance with sections 77 and 78 of the Copyright, Designs and Patents Act 1988.

All rights reserved. No part of this publication may be reproduced, stored in a retrieval system or transmitted in any form or by any means, electronic, mechanical, photocopying, recording or otherwise, without the prior permission of the publishers.

Any person who commits any unauthorised act in relation to this publication may be liable to criminal prosecution and civil claims for damages.

This is a work of fiction. Names, characters, businesses, places, events, locales and incidents are either the products of the author's imagination or used in a fictitious manner. Any resemblance to actual persons, living or dead, or actual events is purely coincidental.

A CIP catalogue record for this title is available from the British Library.

ISBN 9781398400566 (Paperback)
ISBN 9781398401303 (ePub e-book)

www.austinmacauley.com

First Published 2022
Austin Macauley Publishers Ltd®
1 Canada Square
Canary Wharf
London
E14 5AA

Many thanks to: the staff at Austin Macauley; my cousins Linda, Shelagh and Janet; my dear friends Andrea, Anita, Ann, Beverley, Catherine, Elaine, Helen and the "real" Jane; and, most of all, my wonderful husband who has supported me throughout this journey.

Table of Contents

Chapter 1	12
Chapter 2	29
Chapter 3	34
Chapter 4	43
Chapter 5	48
Chapter 6	60
Chapter 7	64
Chapter 8	78
Chapter 9	83
Chapter 10	89
Chapter 11	95
Chapter 12	121
Chapter 13	127
Chapter 14	133
Chapter 15	157
Chapter 16	171

'But O for the touch of a vanish'd hand'
—Tennyson

Chapter 1

I never believed in ghosts, of course I didn't, well that is until last October but it was not until December that things got really out of hand.

"Do you know Mrs Gillian Morris?"

D.C. Kirsty Cameron was a petite blonde with bobbed hair and a no-nonsense, humourless manner. Despite her name, there was no charming Celtic lilt to her accent. I told her that a Mrs Gillian Morris was the school secretary and that she had not come into work nor was she answering her home phone.

"Is this her?"

She asked thrusting a photo driving licence inside an evidence bag towards me. There were blood spatters in the bottom right-hand corner.

"Yes. Is that blood? Look what's happened? Has she been in an accident?"

DC Cameron put away the licence and continued, "The woman you have identified as Mrs Gillian Morris fell under the 9.08 Inverness express train. She left a note addressed to you in her handbag which was recovered near the waiting room wall."

She pulled another evidence bag from her briefcase.

"We would like you to open it in police presence and read it aloud please then it will be kept in evidence until the Inquest."

She handed me a pair of latex gloves and then the bag containing the note. There was no doubt in my mind that the note was from Gillian, she had a very precise italic style of writing. Every letter, perfectly formed and equal in height, was spelling out my name. Whatever was inside the envelope was not going to reflect well on me.

I was the one who gave her the final warning. I was the one determined to be rid of her. Was I also the one who had driven her to suicide?

"Slit it across the top with a letter opener please. We may wish to check for DNA on the gummed section in case someone else sealed the envelope."

I told DC Cameron I thought it was highly unlikely anyone, but Gillian had anything to do with the note because of the idiosyncratic handwriting but I picked up the paua shell letter opener Mayrene had sent me from New Zealand, slit the envelope and removed a single sheet of white writing paper.

"Read it aloud please."

My eye had already run down the first paragraph, it left me completely baffled. I began to read it aloud, *"He has chosen you. I realised it that night you came to the party at my house, when he played the piano for you and laid his hand upon your shoulder. He is yours now and I have nothing further to live for."*

"I have left my will with MacCreith and Scott in Bridge Street. The house is yours; you have to accept it. I have left the dog locked in the house to make sure you have to go inside as soon as possible."

"He is waiting for you. He is cursed already but with my last breath, I curse you."

Gillian Mary Morris

DC Cameron took back the envelope and the letter and sealed them back in the evidence bag.

"So, who is this man you were both involved with?"

The whole thing was so utterly bizarre I didn't know what to say.

"I have no idea. She was obviously even more mentally unbalanced than even I suspected."

DC Cameron looked at me like she expected me to come out with a lie like that.

"Honestly, I do not know what she is talking about!"

Then I remembered reading somewhere that liars always say 'honestly' at the start of a sentence. DC Cameron sighed.

"Let's start at the beginning, shall we? What's this about a party? Did you meet this man there?"

"Look can we just establish the fact that there is no man, except obviously in her confused mind!"

DC Cameron made notes in her book.

"So you never attended a party at Mrs Morris' house?"

"I didn't say that. I went to Mrs Morris' house on October 31st for a Halloween Party. I was with my husband and the Chair of Governors and her husband."

DC Cameron wrote furiously.

"And that is where you met this man."

I was starting to think that having a solicitor present might be a good idea.

"For heaven's sake! How many times? There was no man!"

"But you were at the Halloween Party?"

"Yes!"

DC Cameron flicked back through her notes.

"Where were you at 9.08 this morning?"

Any other morning, every other morning, I would have been right there sitting at my desk but this morning of all mornings I had gone back home after the pupils were all in class, to pick up my mobile phone which I had left on the hall table.

"I had popped back home to pick up my mobile phone which I had left on the hall table."

DC Cameron looked grim and wrote in her notebook.

"And your home address is?"

"Waverley House, Castle Hills, Berwick."

DC Cameron looked up from her notes.

"The Castle Hills which leads down to the Railway station?"

"You could describe it like that yes. Look, DC Cameron what are you trying to say? That I pushed my secretary under the Inverness Express? I went from here to my house; I picked up my phone and I came straight back. Check the cameras on the station. You won't see me on them because I was not there."

DC Cameron looked at me from under her eyelids.

"I won't see you on them because Berwick is just a rural station. There are no cameras and the skeleton staff do not man the platforms unless there is a train due to stop at Berwick station. The express does not stop at Berwick. How would you describe your relationship with Mrs Morris?"

I definitely needed a solicitor. I decided to come clean.

"It was not good. In fact, I had given Mrs Morris a final written warning and I had spoken to the Chair of Governors about starting proceedings to terminate her employment here."

DC Cameron wrote in her book.

"When did you issue the warning and discuss terminating her employment?"

I flipped open my diary. "Seventh and twenty third of November respectively."

DC Cameron made a note.

"So after she became aware of your interest in this man?"

I stood up.

"That's it, DC Cameron. I am sorry that any soul feels it necessary to quit this life by their own hand but that was her decision and it had nothing to do with me. Please leave and if you wish to speak to me again arrange an appointment through my solicitor, James Scott of Bridge Street."

DC Cameron rose to leave.

"I am sorry that you do not wish to help the police with their inquiries of your own volition. I would have thought that someone with nothing to hide would not need a solicitor."

"DC Cameron, I have a school to run. Find your own way out."

She left and I picked up the phone and dialled Jim Scott's number.

I stayed at work for the rest of the day but achieved absolutely nothing. I rang Katherine, the Chair of Governors, and let her know about Gillian's death then I rang the Department and let them know in case of negative publicity and to OK a temp. Then I rang the agency and they confirmed that they had someone suitable on the books who could start next day. Other than that, the rest of the day is a fog.

I kept going over and over the night of the party. Of course, I did know what she meant in the note, but still. I started at the beginning and went back through it all.

I took the job as Head of the new Berwick Primary Academy in September last year. The old Head hadn't fancied the move to the new building, neither had most of the Staff, so it was a great opportunity for me to start a new school from scratch with my own hand-picked team.

The architect had said that the new building would reflect the Town's maritime traditions and that 'the exterior of cedar and chrome would be reminiscent of a New England beach house'. In fact, we got pine which is moulding and steel which is rusting already. The atrium is pointless and freezing most of the year. There is no staffroom and the classrooms only have three walls so it is like teaching in the Tower of Babel but the new Staff is superb and we were all pulling together and making the best of it except for Gillian Morris.

Gillian Morris was the Secretary at the old school. She had a temper like a wasp in a bottle and she snapped at everyone like a shark. She made the children cry and was rude to Staff and visitors alike. By October, I had had enough, and I called the Chair of Governors in to tell her that I was going to give Gillian the sack.

The Chair was a jolly middle-aged psychologist called Katherine Bleakley.

"Oh, don't do that!" she pleaded. "Gillian has had a tragic time of it you know. She has only been in Berwick about five years herself and not long after she arrived, her husband fell off a ladder in their new home and died. He broke his neck. Everyone knows this so we all put up with her. Nobody here would want to see Gillian sacked and besides, she is going to ask you to the house for Halloween. John and I go every year to Gillian's for Halloween, you must, must come. It is a genuine haunted house, and everyone wears early Victorian costume, it is extraordinary. Give Gillian the year out and if you want, we will say good-bye to her in the summer, okay?"

Katherine was right about the invitation, there was a black-edged envelope in my pigeon-hole requesting the pleasure. My husband Tom did not want to go any more than I did but I ordered a couple of outfits from the internet, and we were pleased with them when they came. He had a vintage tailcoat and waistcoat rig, and I had a ball gown in champagne satin. I put my hair up and wore some long gloves I had had at university and off we went. Big mistake! Biggest mistake of our lives as it turned out.

Gillian's house is one of the six-bedroomed Georgian houses on the Old Quay Walls constructed of dark grey, granite blocks. The original eighteenth century iron torch sconces still adorn the steps. Gillian had lit them. Little flames guttered in the chill night breeze.

The entrance hall was impressive, black and white chequer-board marble tiles and a grand circular staircase which swept up into darkness. It was clean and not unlike similar entrance halls of its era. Katherine and John had come with us, and Katherine nudged me as Gillian took our coats away.

"This is where the husband died," she whispered.

I could not imagine wanting to keep a house in those circumstances and said so to Katherine.

"Got to, nobody in Berwick would ever buy it and that's a fact!"

I asked her why not. It clearly needed a lot of work but the view down the river to Lindisfarne must be stunning in daylight.

"Oh, it is," said Katherine. "It is the history of the house that puts local people off. Gillian's husband was not the first to meet with an unexplained accident in this house."

Katherine shut up as Gillian returned. She was dressed as a housekeeper in a black gown with a silver chatelaine at her waist. She led us to double doors at the left of the entrance and pushed them back together.

The scene which met my eyes was unforgettable. It was such a collision of rot and luxury. I can't really explain it better than that. At first, the room seemed completely black. It was lit only by a fire roaring in the ox-blood marble fireplace and a pair of solid gold filigree candelabra. The high darkness of the ceiling swallowed most of the brightness before it reached more than a yard above the table. The floor was bare and ingrained with centuries of dust. The walls were covered in brown, embossed leather with the remains of gilding gleaming dully in the candlelight. Toledo leather, originally cream and gold according to Gillian. She began to explain the plans she and her husband had for its restoration but tailed off and walked away into the next room closing the doors behind her. A long table ran down the centre of the room. There was no cloth, just the dark oak boards but on those bare boards sat the most exquisite Meissen dinner service: green and gold borders, bone white centres, hand-painted roses and tiny, rainbow-coloured butterflies.

I made a joke to Katherine that we were paying our secretary too much, but Katherine said that the Meissen service, the candelabra, in fact all the furnishings came with the house.

"I for one wouldn't want any of it!" she added.

I told Katherine not to be so mysterious and to hit me with the details of this allegedly haunted house and she was about to tell all when Gillian came in with a huge silver tureen of soup.

The dinner was delicious and all the better for eating it off the best china I had ever seen outside of a museum. Gillian disappeared through the doors again and we all gravitated towards the fire as there was not only the smell but also the clammy feel of damp in the room. It was then that Tom noticed the dog basket in the chimney corner and its occupant, a shivering greyhound. Tom is something of a dog whisperer but when he bent to stroke this dog it growled at the back of its throat and stared at us all with its dark eyes on stalks.

Gillian returned with a framed letter, its paper yellow with age, its brown ink fading, she handed it to me and asked me to read it aloud saying that it outlined some of the history of the house. I began to read what amounted to a deathbed confession of murder.

It was written by the first owner of the house. He had believed that his daughter's Polish piano tutor, Count Stanislav Beretsky, was after her affections. Times were hard and there was no difficulty finding four men to waylay the pianist and beat him. There had been a special instruction to break his hands. The pianist had staggered back to Berwick, to the house on the Old Quay Walls but he was denied admittance. It was winter. He died on the doorstep.

Silence fell as I stopped reading and, out of the dark, a hand grabbed my left shoulder. I can feel it still. It was the heavy hand of a man, the weight of long fingers, the pressure of fingertips. I turned into darkness and no one was there. We searched the room and Tom laughed and said it was imagination but then from the piano in the corner of the room the clear, beautiful Chopin prelude, expertly played. Even Gillian looked shocked though she tried to say it was a recording for effect, she admitted later in her letter that it wasn't.

We left the house soon after, but I felt an oddness, an uneasiness, a dread that clung to me like a wet shirt. I had taken something from the house away with me, something I did not want.

Normally, I go home about six, but I had made an appointment with my solicitor Jim Scott for four thirty so, as soon as the bell went and the parents had cleared, I ran for the car and just drove around in a daze, finding myself in the Bridge Street car-park about quarter past four. I got out and headed the few yards down the street to Jim's office.

Jim had shared a flat with my friend Jane and me in our final year at university. He was and is tall, dark and handsome and devastatingly charming. He and Jane had a thing going at one point, but it never came to anything. I wondered why I never succumbed to the charm etc. but then when you have seen your flatmate first thing with tatty hair and a hangover, wearing only a pair of greying underpants with one bollock hanging out, it kind of ruins the glamour.

I stepped into his business premises. It had that smell of old paper and dust that the offices of old firms always have. Jim had been snapped up by some flash firm in London straight from Uni and done rather well but the sudden death of his father had dragged him back to Berwick to sort out the family firm. MacCreith and Scott had been in business in Berwick since the late 1700s and Jim's secretary Mrs Kerry looked like she had started there around about that date. In truth, she looked like a mummified monkey. She showed me into Jim's office and said he was down in the cellars where the deeds and wills were kept, and he would join me shortly.

My bag was unaccountably heavy, so I put it down on the floor and sat down to wait for Jim. He took an age but eventually swept in, hugged me and plonked himself down on the swivel chair behind his desk.

"I've had a word with Gregor Morgan, the Chief Inspector for Berwick and he has given your police detective constable a flea in her ear so you shouldn't have anymore of her nonsense from now on. There will of course be an inquest although it is not likely to be any time soon and if you are called, it will be solely for the purpose of testifying to the state of her mind in recent weeks. So that is that part. The next part is this will and so forth."

He patted the thick bundle of legal documents he had brought in with him.

"This is Gillian Morris's will leaving everything to you and these are the deeds of the house which, as you can see, are bulky old numbers. All hand-written from the early 1800s when the house was built. There is also a confession to murder in here."

I nodded.

"Oh yes, I know about that, the original owner's confession about arranging the killing of the piano teacher. Gillian made me read it out loud at that Halloween party."

Jim looked puzzled.

"No, my pet, this is Gillian's confession to murdering her husband."

"What?"

"Quite. She reckons she waited until he was up a ladder by the upstairs landing, and she pushed him over the balustrade. One look at that and no jury in the land would convict you for driving her to suicide, she was clearly crackers and homicidal to boot. So, all in all, a bit of a windfall for you. What are you going to do with it? I take it you don't want to live in it. Shall I put it on the market for you? Might get some ignorant, greedy developer from down South snapping it up for say £300k."

I pointed out that it might be best to wait until the woman had had a decent burial before flogging off her house and its contents and continued, "Anyway, I don't want it or anything in it. I want to give it to the National Trust, lock stock and barrel."

Jim was amazed.

"Whoa. Look, this has been a stressful day, Kate. You go home to Capt. Tom and talk it over with him. We could be talking half a million quid here by the time all the furniture, plate and so on are thrown in."

"No, Jim. I can't talk to Tom; he is deep sea until next Tuesday. Anyway, I have made up my mind. First thing in the morning, I want you to get rid of it, all of it. I don't even like the idea of owning it overnight."

Jim sighed.

"You surely don't believe in all that ghost/curse claptrap, do you? Come on Kate, you are an educated woman. This is a golden opportunity for you and Tom. I tell you what, I'll start on it tomorrow afternoon, but it will take months to transfer it to the National Trust, if they will even take it on. Go home and think about it."

I banged my fists on the table.

"No! There must be something you can do to get this house from around my neck as soon as possible Jim, as soon as possible!"

He held his hands up.

"All right, Kate, all right, but I think you are making a big boo-boo. I'll put it into a trust tomorrow morning in the firm's name and you can come in and sign it after school. How's that? I still hope that somebody will talk sense into you in the meantime but, if you come in tomorrow to sign it, so be it. What have you done about the dog?"

I had forgotten all about the bloody dog!

Jim shook a bunch of heavy five-inch-long keys from a manila envelope, they looked like something that would lock up the Tower of London.

"Are you going around there now? You'll have to notify the police of your intent to enter the premises in case there are any further clues there about Mrs Morris' demise. I'll come with you if you like."

I told him I would like. I certainly had no intention of ever crossing that threshold ever again. He was my over-priced solicitor he could go in and get the dog. I asked him to ring the people at BARK, the Berwick Animal Rescue Kennels, they would take the dog away and find it a home. I definitely didn't want the scrawny, bad-tempered mutt. Jim made the calls.

It was only a short walk from Jim's office to the house. We stood outside on the pavement; I did not want to even mount the steps. I stood by the Elizabethan town wall and looked across the river to Spittal where the old chimney from the derelict salmon canning factory pointed at a leaden sky. The evening was the usual winter mix of gloom and drizzle and by the time, all were assembled my coat was soaked and I was beginning to shiver though possibly not from the chill air alone.

Last to arrive was the sulky DC Cameron and two burly constables carrying the sort of battering ram you see on TV reality cop shows.

"My colleagues and I will enter the building first with this gentleman from BARK. You cannot enter until I give the all clear. There could be vital clues in here as to why Mrs Morris committed suicide and I don't want you tampering with them," said the charming Kirsty. Jim spoke for me.

"I believe you have been warned once today already DC Cameron about the attitude you have taken towards my client. Change your tone or you will find yourself skulking back to your Inspector to ask for a search warrant and in the meantime Mrs Webster will have free let and use of her own property. I remind you that you are here as a courtesy only and we are at perfect liberty to ask you and your colleagues to leave."

Kirsty said nothing and looked even more sulky, casting murderous looks my way.

"Right then," said Jim. "Now that we understand each other shall we go in and get this over with?"

Jim walked up to the massive oak door, pulled the bunch of long, rusty, hand-made keys from his overcoat pocket and placed the largest in the keyhole which was a brass affair in the shape of a lion's mouth.

The keys fit but did not open the door. Everyone except me had a go at jiggling the key. The BARK man jogged back to his van and brought back some WD40, but it did no good, so the two burly policemen stepped up. They took hold of the ram, one on each side and battered the door, once, twice, three times but it did no good. They were about to try again when suddenly the door opened of its own accord. The handle turned and the door swung with an impressive squeal.

Suddenly, DC Cameron seemed less keen to enter the premises.

"That handle turned. There must be someone inside. Harry, you go around the back. Take those keys in case the back gate is locked." Jim threw him the keys. "Dean you go in and be careful."

Dean gingerly shoved the door open a little wider and leapt back like a cat as something in the dark hall clanged to the ground. He shone his torch back and forth flicking images briefly into view: the chequered floor, the winding staircase, the closed mahogany doors, the chandelier and the metal umbrella stand which had caused the clang by throwing itself unaccountably to the chequered floor.

"Where did she keep the dog?" asked the BARK man clearly not keen to go rambling all over this ghastly pile.

"It was in a basket near the fireplace in the dining room the last time I saw it," I told him.

DC Cameron had turned on a totally inadequate torch of her own it projected a totally inadequate gleam about the strength of a birthday candle, but it succeeded in locating the light switch. She flicked it with a sigh of relief. It did no good. I had to smile. The efficient Gillian must have paid a final bill to the power company and had the supply cut off.

There was nothing for it but to search the place by torchlight. I fished in my handbag and pulled out the massive LED torch I kept in my bag in case the lights went out in school and I handed it to Jim.

"I should have known!" He smiled. "Old Ever-ready rides again!"

I had gained the nickname Ever-ready one weekend in our final year at uni. We all went on a weekend break to a self-catering farmhouse in the middle of nowhere. I had saved the day by supplying from my handbag, bootlaces, 15-amp fuses and a gas mantle.

I had mounted the steps to hand Jim the torch, I was not prepared to go any further, but I peered through the door as the four of them set off through the total blackness to find the dog. Jim took the lead.

"The dining room is the first door on the left," I called.

They approached the door. Dean stretched out his hand to turn the handle and then we heard them. Clear ringing footsteps tramping slowly towards us from the rear of the house. Worse, the tall figure of a man emerging from the gloom.

All torches swung in unison towards the cadaverous face.

"Harry, you bloody idiot! I nearly shat myself!" yelled Dean.

"What? There was nobody around the back, so I used the keys to let myself in! Have you found the dog?"

The BARK man suddenly remembered he had to be somewhere else in quarter of an hour, so Dean grabbed the door handle again and threw open the door. A blaze of light and sound met them as the candles on the chandelier burst into foot high flames and that bloody Chopin prelude kicked off at a crazy pace from the piano in the corner where no pianist sat.

The rest stood stunned, but the BARK man made a grab for the dog which was curled up in its basket as before. Suddenly, the candles went out, the piano thrummed into silence and, once more in pitch blackness, the rest ran after the BARK man into the street. PC Harry turned to lock the door only to have the door slammed in his face so ferociously that it knocked him down the stairs.

The dog was dead. The BARK man shook his head and said he had never seen anything like it.

Chapter 2

The following day was the last Friday of the school term, so all the kids were dressed as various Disney and Harry Potter characters. The Staff put on a pantomime in the morning followed by Year 3 nativity and carols then each class had a party in their room in the afternoon with a buffet lunch and early finish. We had thought about cancelling all of it, but the kids were oblivious, if not glad, that Gillian was gone and the Staff thought it unfair to deprive them of their Christmas fun, it would do no good for Gillian.

By 2.30pm, all was cleared up and everyone was gone for the holidays. Being an academy, we were able to choose our own term dates and the Board of Governors had decided upon a Christmas holiday of six weeks, one week at Easter and a month in the summer. The thinking behind this was that it would save on the heating bill, cut down the risk of kids being knocked over in the dark or hurting themselves slipping on ice and suing the school. It was win-win, so we broke for six weeks starting that day Friday 4th December.

I had taken home the bundle of papers Jim Scott had given me the day before and by 3pm, I was curled up in an armchair at home with a cup of coffee and the papers on my knee. I started with the original deeds of the house. They were hand-written on really thick vellum-type stuff with an illuminated first letter at the top and seals at the bottom. Very boring to read and not for the first time I was glad that I hadn't gone in for the law. All I learnt from them was the name of the house, Cyprus House, and the original owner, James Knox. Other papers gave the names of the subsequent owners, none of whom had kept the property longer than a year, culminating with the names of Gillian and her husband. Gillian and her husband had new deeds drawn up as the law required when they bought the place Jim had those and copies had been sent by computer to the Land Registry.

I kept the confession written by James Knox until last. It was just as I remembered it from that night Gillian handed it to me, but it was no longer in a frame and I saw for the first time something scrawled along the bottom on part of it that had been folded over to make it fit the frame it had been in. The scrawl was in the same handwriting, James Knox' handwriting, but as if written in a hurry or under extreme stress. It said, "I was wrong. God forgive me. What I have done was for all our good even hers. God have mercy on us."

Obviously, he meant that having the piano teacher killed was for his daughter's own good, Knox clearly thought this guy had designs on his daughter, was after her money or had sexually assaulted her or both but he had already said that in the body of the letter strange that he felt moved to say it again.

I put his confession and Gillian's on top of the pile and put the lot away in a box file ready for Jim Scott to hand them to the police. I had hoped that Gillian paid off the house with the insurance money from her husband's death which would be fraud, since she killed him, and you cannot profit from crime, or everybody would be doing it! I thought the

30

insurance company would repossess the house and I would be off the hook, but the Morrises had sold a house in London and bought Cyprus House outright. I was stuck with it temporarily. But I did not have to have anything to do with it in my house. I picked up my car keys and set off for MacCreith and Scott so that I could sign the Trust papers and Jim could start getting rid of it for me.

I parked my car at the top of the Town and walked down past the shops doing good trade in the fast-vanishing light, only twenty shopping days left until Christmas. The Civic Fathers always did a good job on the High Street, it was looped across with coloured lights and each shop had a real fir tree hung above its door with rainbow fairy lights twinkling. If I could get rid of this accursed house this afternoon, maybe I could get back into my usual Christmassy mood. All in all, I was quite hopeful when I turned the corner into Bridge Street.

The road was completely blocked by fire engines and their hoses. An ambulance stood at the door of MacCreith and Scott. Its back door was open, and Jim was sitting on its tailgate. His shoulders were wrapped in a waffle blanket, and he had an oxygen mask over his nose and mouth. They were bringing his secretary out on a stretcher, and she was coughing as a result of the smoke which was still curling out of the offices. I rushed along the street towards Jim only to be halted by the burly arm of Dean, the young policeman from the previous night.

"Can't go through here at the moment, madam," he said.

"Dean, it's me, Mrs Webster, from last night remember? I just want to see if Jim is all right."

Before Dean could tell me to push off, Jim spotted me and called to Dean to let me through, an effort which made him cough and suck on his oxygen mask with gusto. I rushed along to the ambulance and sat down by Jim on the tailgate.

"What on earth has happened?" I asked.

Jim glanced from side to side to be sure that nobody could overhear then whispered, "It's the deeds belonging to that house of yours!" He sucked in a long breath of oxygen. "I went down to the cellar to get them out of the filing cabinet, all stone cellar, metal filing cabinet and as I opened the drawer they were in and began to lift them out…" He had a coughing fit, and the ambulance man gave me a look, but Jim waved him away.

"…As I began to lift them out, the bloody things spontaneously combusted!" He took another deep breath and continued, "Not only them either, suddenly every drawer in the cellar flew open and started blazing. Half the property deeds in Berwick were in there not to mention the wills! All gone up in smoke!" He coughed some more. "You were right, Kate. Nothing good is going to come of that house, but I'm afraid you are stuck with it until we get a copy of the deeds from the Land Registry in Durham."

I reminded him that I had the original deeds, but he pointed out they were no longer valid and new ones would have to be fetched from Durham.

I told him not to worry about it and fished in my bag to get a bottle of water. While he was drinking it, I went off to ask after his secretary, she was fine, mostly shock at seeing Jim emerging from the inferno of the cellar in a halo of smoke and flames. They were both to be kept in hospital for observation overnight, but a full recovery was expected. Jim promised to let me know when he was released so that I could fetch him, then the ambulance man slammed the doors and drove away.

The firemen rolled up their hoses. I stood in the dark street staring at the smoke smudged office front and wondered how long I was going to be stuck with the place now.

Chapter 3

By morning, I had a plan. Tom always tells me to play to my strengths, so I decided to do what I do best, possibly the only thing I ever have been any good at…research it to buggery and beyond! As it happened, I had agreed to swap days volunteering at the Berwick Archive. I made up my mind to know mine enemy by finding out as much as I could from the records about Cyprus House, the Knox family and the bloody piano player who was making my life a misery.

On the way to the Archives, I had popped into the adjacent graveyard. No one had been buried there since the early years of Victoria's reign, but it had been the only burial spot in Berwick at the time of the piano teacher's murder. As I expected, the cast of characters were all buried there with the notable exception of the teacher himself but then being Polish, he was most likely Catholic so buried across the river in the Catholic cemetery in Tweedmouth.

At one time, my idea of a great day out was a trip to an old cemetery like this one. It appealed to the historian in me to spot when the epidemics had hit, when the Indian wars or fishing disasters had taken their toll. My favourite was the hilltop cemetery in Tynemouth in the shadow of the abbey ruins where lie three ancient kings and the man who held the lantern for the burial of Sir John Moore at Corunna. Recent events, however, had put me off lone spooky places and my aim was to get in and out of this one as fast as possible. The cemetery wrapped itself around the bleak, white stone Presbyterian Church, a grand, austere pile with its plain glass windows facing the North Sea beyond the Town Walls.

It was mostly overgrown, and I had to struggle through a wilderness of wet, decaying weeds to get to the part of it relating to the 1830s. I had an unnerving feeling that I was being watched. Despite looking behind me every five seconds, however, I saw no one and, let's face it, who would want to be standing staring in a dripping, old graveyard on a dim December afternoon? And yet the feeling remained.

For a graveyard facing the merciless North Sea, the headstones were mostly in good nick and still legible. Headstones back then gave a lot more information than we bother with now, names obviously but also addresses, cause of death, place of death, names of relatives. I read my way past drowned sailors and infant mortalities, counting back the years to the 1830s. It did not take me long to find the large pink granite obelisk that marked the last resting place of the man who put the contract out on the piano teacher. I made notes of the inscriptions and headed for the Archive.

Berwick Archive is situated in the old Council Offices in Wallace Green. It is one of Berwick's more modern buildings having only been there since the reign of Charles I. It is made of local stone and has the appearance of a baronial hunting lodge with its twenty one Elizabethan-style chimneys and carved stone crest above the studded door.

It holds court records, borough records and, what I was after, copies of the *Berwick Courant* founded in 1815. Luckily for me, the service is no longer supported by the County Council and the archive is run by volunteers of which I had been one since July so when I turned up for my shift I found only Norma Miles, another volunteer, in the building. The Council itself had moved to Ashington years before as a money-saving measure which of course had cost a fortune and saved no money at all.

Norma is a tall and elegant woman in her early fifties but doesn't look her age. She can give you a shock emerging from the gloom of the stacks as she is vintage mad and can be got up as anything from an eighteenth-century lady to a Flapper depending on what re-enactment is going on that week. This week was wartime WAF. Her black hair was caught up in a victory roll, her genuine WAF uniform cinched in with the right leather belt for the period.

We chatted about the latest gossip, of course she wanted the details about Gillian, and I told her to help set the record straight i.e., that contrary to popular rumour I did not kill her. There were no readers booked in, there rarely were, so Norma checked her hair and wished me luck as she waved me goodbye.

I almost ran to the stacks and heaved out the great, green, leather-bound copies of the Courant for 1833. No microfiche here, let alone digital copy.

I was alone in the building. The thought made me shiver and I determined to read fast and get out faster. I opened the great green tome and let its heavy leather cover bang dust into the silence of the deserted building.

I knew from James Knox' gravestone that he had died in 1835 aged 45 of heart failure. Two years earlier his 15-year-old daughter, Lydia, had drowned in May of 1833, presumably suicide, because of the inscription under her name, 'Near her home, Cyprus House unaccountably swept out to sea'. My plan was to start in December of 1832 to check for mention of the piano teacher and details of Knox' wife Eliza who 'Fell to her death from the captain's walk of Cyprus House' March of 1833 and go on from there if need be. I was in for a shock.

I began to notice a pattern in the January of 1833. I had started with births, marriages and deaths because it was Mrs Knox' death I was most interested in, but before I came to her it became obvious that a high number of 15-year-old local girls were dying, sometimes two a month. That in itself not especially odd for the times or even today as some diseases like meningitis seem to cut a swathe through young adults, so I looked for signs of epidemics of that and diphtheria, smallpox and scarlet fever all easily caught at school that could and did wipe out whole class sets of children back in the day. There was no mention anywhere of epidemics. I noted down their details. Of the six girls who died over a period of three months, there was one burnt to death, two killed in a boating accident, one accidentally poisoned and one fell downstairs. I nearly jumped out of my skin as the clang of some heavy metal tool hitting the floor rang out behind me. The noise was coming from the stacks. I approached the door.

Why was I trembling? There was no one here but me. I was sitting in the room with the only door to the outside world so no one had come in and Norma assured me there was nobody in the stacks when she left. I put my hand out to grasp the door handle but pulled back when the clang came again. This time, a series of clanging noises like someone beating two iron bars together: bang, bang, bang, a shuddering rhythmic clang. It stopped. I reached for the handle again only to see it suddenly turn a spiky white as sharp frost crystals spread across it. Suddenly, my breath was standing in the air and the temperature in the room was plummeting.

This was ridiculous, I told myself, trying not to think about all those fright-night documentaries where some dizzy blonde screams a lot and says the temperature is dropping like a stone. But the temperature was dropping like a stone.

I grabbed the handle and yanked open the door. The din began again and in the dim light, I was almost sure I could see a long wrench rising and falling, moving by itself as it beat and beat the stopcock on the wall. As I peered into the gloom, a jet of water burst forwards, soaking the precious records and starting to flood the floor. I grabbed as many of the green tomes as I could, but they were so heavy I could only manage two at a time and the water was rising so fast in the tiny room. Wading through it, I went as fast as I could into the next room dropped them on the table and rushed back only to see the books apparently hurling themselves off their safe shelves and into the foaming water. I flung myself back into the room and caught hold of St Andrew's Parish Register in mid-air. Whatever unseen force was hanging on to the other end of it had some strength to it. I ended up heaving with all my might, determined that this evil bugger wasn't going to win this one when all of a sudden it let go and me and the book splashed into the yard deep icy water. I grabbed another book in passing and waded out to the anteroom.

I turned back to the stacks. Two steps would bring me back into the stack, but the door slammed shut as I approached and no amount of yanking on it would make it give. I grabbed my bag and flung open my phone to call the fire brigade, knowing it was already too late for all the handwritten council minutes and church records, their inky secrets washed away forever.

As I sat on the table in the anteroom waiting for the fire brigade with the few precious, dripping, tomes of the *Courant*, I thought about the spate of deaths in an era of common child mortality and no questions asked with no forensic scientist or keen pathologist to catch him out.

Shivering with cold and anger, I began to wonder if the piano-playing Count I was dealing with was a serial killer, an early nineteenth century serial killer, but a psycho all the same. Had he killed all of those girls and even from beyond the grave had driven Gillian to murder and suicide? What would he do next and why had he chosen me? Then the sane part of me told me to pull myself together and stop talking rubbish, but the wrench had moved unaided, and I had sensed the presence of something both wicked and determined pulling on the tome in the stacks.

The fire brigade arrived promptly, unfortunately for me, DC Kirsty Cameron turned up with them. The firemen pumped the place out in no time but, as I suspected, the damage was devastating to the records. DC Kirsty Cameron ignored me and brushed past me deliberately to enter the stacks. After a few words with the fireman, she condescended to acknowledge my presence. The long wrench was in her hand.

"Well, well, well. Mrs Webster at the scene of another crime. Murder and arson not enough for you in one week? Now we have vandalism and criminal damage!"

She was loving this.

"I believe that my solicitor has already spoken to your superiors about your attitude towards me DC Cameron. I would not push your luck if I were you."

She let the wrench lift and drop into her palm as if she would love to beat me over the head with it.

"Well, you won't get away with it this time because I have the smoking gun so to speak; the wrench you used to do the damage!"

I sighed, shaking my head, whilst removing my bone-dry gloves from my bag.

"Look, Kirsty, here are my gloves, totally dry. I insist, by the way, that you check all the bins in Berwick so that you can see that I have not tried to dispose of any other gloves because you will find that my fingerprints are not on that wrench."

"No! Because you had loads of time to wipe them off before we got here!"

"No, my pet, because I have never touched that thing in my life."

I put on my gloves, slung my bag over my shoulder and left the building with as much dignity as my squelching shoes would allow.

I left Kirsty fuming but unable to pin anything on me and no doubt screaming in her head.

"I'll get you, Kate Webster, and your little dog too!"

My phone buzzed. I had a text from Jim saying he was ready to be collected from Borders General Hospital. I returned home to change and dry off then I texted him to say I was on my way. I took the quick route, the A698 and I was in Galashiels in an hour. Jim was waiting for me by the front doors. His hair was standing on end, and he was wearing the smoke-damaged suit and shirt he had worn yesterday.

"Thanks, Kate," he said as he closed the car door.

"What gives with the scruffy suit? Did Lucienne not visit you last night?"

Lucienne was his much younger, modellesque, French girlfriend.

"No. She buggered off back to France last month."

That was a shame, Lucienne was clever and feisty and just what he needed.

"Marriage thing again?"

"Yup."

Fair enough, he had been in a fire and spent a night with no sleep, which is a pre-requisite of the modern hospital, but even so his blood pressure was clearly through the roof. I told him so.

"The days of all-nighters and putting it about are now behind you. It is time you settled down before nobody will have you. The bloom has decidedly gone off your rose my old china."

"Thanks, Kate. May I remind you it is your fault that I was nearly fried to death yesterday?"

"How was that my fault?"

"It was your bloody house."

"Now you can see why I want rid! Anyway, you ain't heard nothing yet."

I told him what had happened in the Archives and what I had found out in the cemetery.

"Had you told me this two days ago I would have sent for a psychiatrist, but not only is there no explanation for the fire in my office but also what the hell happened in that creepy house? The self-opening doors, the ten-foot candle flames and the petrified dog! This is some freaky shit, Kate. You know who you have to call, and I don't mean Ghostbusters."

He meant Jane. I rang her and left a voice message but the recording on her phone said she was in Abu Dhabi until the end of the week.

Chapter 4

Berwick had never seen anything like Jane. She is five feet ten inches tall in bare feet, size 8 in clothes and everything she wears costs more than the take-home pay of anyone in Berwick or the Borders generally come to that. She is the daughter of money and made plenty of her own as, and here I kid you not, a brain surgeon. Not just any brain surgeon you understand, oh no, brain surgeon on speed dial for the Royal Family, well, quite a number of Royal Families actually. She had long since given up working nine to five and just popped in to help with especially tricky cases, so she was free to help me unless her work mobile rang.

You may think that by this point I had sent for Jane to give my brain the once-over because I realised, I was going mad but no. Jane has a talent outside that of a run-of-the-mill genius. Jane is…well she can… I never know how to tell people this without making them burst out laughing. In a nutshell, Jane talks to dead people and they talk back to her. All through university while I spent the holidays working in a hot, smelly, chocolate factory churning out chocolate frogs, she was touring Europe or the States, all expenses paid, packing out theatres with her one-woman show.

She stepped down from the train slinging a Louis Vuitton bag onto the platform before her and pulling on her designer Afghan coat. Seventies chic is in again she tells me.

"It's always bloody freezing here, Kate. I don't know why you insist on living here!"

"And hello to you too, Jane."

She kissed both my cheeks.

"I should be able to stay until this is sorted out, but you realise if the phone goes, I'll have to vanish."

I told her I realised the terms and we headed for the carpark and home. Over tea and home-made lemon cake, her favourite, I filled her in on the story so far. All she said was, "Hmmm." Then she got up and fished in her bag. She pulled out two silver egg cups.

"The house needs cleansing. Your feeling that you brought something from that house with you was spot on. Hang on a minute."

She got up and started banging the eggcups together in each of the corners of the room.

"What the hell are you doing?"

"I'm using the purity of the sound to clear the house of unwanted energy."

"Jane, this ghost, spirit or whatever has so far burnt down Jim's office and destroyed most of the archive material of the entire town. Do you really think he is going to be scared of an eggcup?"

Jane moved from corner to corner of the room.

"Two eggcups. You are supposed to use Tibetan singing bowls, but they are so bulky to cart about and I have found these silver eggcups produce exactly the same tone. I had the Music Department at work check them out. This is very scientific you know, once you get past the fact that they have Humpty Dumpty engraved on the front. Now you open all the windows while I ring these in every corner of the house."

She rang them in every corner then let me close the windows again. I know this is going to sound dumb but there was a difference in the house. As if a heaviness had departed and a clean, lightness in the air had taken its place.

"What's for dinner? I'm starving. You can tell me what you found out thus far about our mystery man while I have a nice glass of wine."

What I knew about our mystery man, the piano teacher, was next to nothing. I knew his name, that he was Polish and played the piano. A trip to the Catholic graveyard at Tweedmouth had proved fruitless as they had no record of anyone Polish buried there until the 1940s. I had, however, come to a grim conclusion regarding the possible whereabouts of his remains.

The original owner of the house was James Knox. His brother, Dr Robert Knox, was Keeper of the Museum of Medical Surgery attached to Edinburgh University, this was an honorary position with a lot of kudos and a small stipend. The post was offered to the Chief Surgeon in the Medical Academy at the time.

"What does any of that have to do with our pianist?"

I sighed.

"You are not going to like this, Jane."

"Try me."

"Ever heard of Burke and Hare?"

"Oh no! He got his brother to cut up the pianist in an anatomy class and thereby dispose of the body!"

I nodded.

"Yup. His brother cut him up in front of an audience of medical students and other voyeurs with time on their hands. He is written up as, 'unknown Polish vagrant run over by cart in Berwick upon Tweed whilst inebriated'. As far as I can see, what was left of him was burnt in the University incinerator and that is not the worst of it."

Jane took a swig of her wine.

"There is worse than being beaten up, left to freeze and bleed to death on Mr Knox's doorstep, then being cut up in front of a crowd of onlookers and flung into an incinerator?"

I nodded.

"Before he went to the incinerator, Knox's brother had him flayed and tanned and his skin turned into a variety of notebooks, wallets and card cases which were sold as souvenirs to said onlookers at future dissections. Only two remain in circulation. One of which was sold in 1988 for £1050 to a ghost tour company in Edinburgh and the only other known about is on display in the Surgeon's Hall Museum, Edinburgh."

Jane shook her head in disbelief.

"You begin to see why his ghost is so pissed off." She put down her glass and stood up. "We have to get them back, the bits I mean. The ghost tour company, if still in existence, will sell theirs especially if I turn up with a facsimile, an obscene amount of cash and a solicitor's letter swearing that I will never breathe a word about the swap. The university is another matter, archivists never let anything, no matter how pointless, out of their bony grip."

Jane knew very well that I had trained and worked as an archivist for several years before going in for teaching when my daughter Sophia was born.

"It is worse than that," I said. "The museum is closed for eighteen months for renovation. They have a lottery grant."

Jane thought for a moment.

"Then we either steal it or I have to sleep with whoever is the current Head of Surgery at Edinburgh. I just hope it isn't that slimy Donail McHaill."

I could hardly bring myself to tell her that it was indeed Old Slimy himself. Jane went off to find the gin and I went on to the Trainline website to book two tickets to Edinburgh next day. I would make enquiries about public access to their collection whilst the building was under repair and if necessary, visit the School of Architecture and photograph the plans of the museum building for burglary purposes. I did not envy Jane.

Chapter 5

The Museum of Medical Surgery is on Nicholson Street in Edinburgh. You can't miss it, it has a massive portico supported by six impressive, grey marble, Doric columns. It was founded in 1505, according to Google, and it contains numerous collections. The upper floor of the building, designed by William Playfair, houses the pathology museum but it is only accessible to guided tours. The lower gallery is more open to all and houses the history of surgery in the city. Luckily for me they were having a temporary Burke and Hare exhibition to pull in the punters who might otherwise have found the on-going lottery work off-putting.

And so it was that the following day Jane and I were in Edinburgh, standing among the tourists and Christmas shoppers with larceny in mind. Jane set off for the bank to withdraw sufficient cash to persuade the tour company to hand over their skin-bound book and I made my way through the drizzle to the Museum of Medical Surgery.

Access through the impressive portico was not possible because of the renovations but a little door to the left of the main entrance showed me straight into an echoey double-height room. White wooden pillars supported an upper gallery, leaving a central hall with eight carrels on each side.

Down the centre of the floor were four octagonal display tables, two at each end, separated by a long, boat-shaped glass display cabinet which contained the Burke and Hare exhibition.

It was lunchtime and the gallery staff seemed to have gone off in search of sandwiches or something because I found myself completely alone. Two long red woollen carpets ran the length of the pale wooden floor either side of the cabinets, so my feet made no sound to disturb the stillness. I scanned the room for CCTV cameras but amazingly, there were none. Presumably, the Trustees thought no one would want the ghoulish exhibits laid out in pickle jars of various sizes on open shelving around the walls. Had they never heard of Goths?

I approached the boat-shaped table. There was a sun-bleached paper sign on it declaring that the table was alarmed. It did not take long to discover the thick, cloth-covered wire tacked along the side of the table. It was a faded maroon colour and had clearly been applied to the Victorian table in the 1930s. Some of the tacks had come loose and it was dangling in several places. That and the fact its Bakelite plug was not plugged in to anything gave me hope that this was going to be easier than I thought.

I began to look at the exhibits in the case: a poster about the trial of Burke and Hare, a paperknife used for the killings, Burke's confession, his death mask and finally the skin-bound book. It was about the size of two DVD cases laid on top of each other. It was a lovely shade of red, a wine colour really, a bit knocked about. It had clearly been used and carried in a pocket by the look of it, scraping against coins and keys and so on. The word 'Execution' was embossed into the top of it.

I quickly looked around. Nobody there. I lifted the lid which, much to my amazement made no sound. Suddenly, I realised I was not wearing my gloves. I had taken them off automatically when I came in from the cold. Should I shut the lid again? If I did, I might miss my chance. I could hear distant conversation. If I didn't, then I would have to grab the book skin to skin. I grabbed it and slammed the lid down on the display case.

I felt hot and prickly and sick and queasy. I dropped the thing into my bag and retched. It was an obscene thing to touch the skin of this pervert, undead monster. I fished my gloves out with two fingers so that I did not have to touch the book again or even brush against it, then I used the gloves to rub down the lid. In case of any CSI involvement, I then squirted some water all over the area from a delicately extracted bottle. I shoved the bottle back into my bag and walked briskly from the Hall, out onto the Street and away.

I had taken the precaution of wearing a wig and cheap outfit bought in Primark en route to the Museum. With a hat and scarf and sunglasses and moonboots, my own mother would not have recognised me. I made for Jenners' and completely changed my clothing in the toilets. I tipped the stolen contents of the Primark overnight bag into my handbag then replaced it with my new purchases, wig and all. The book had tumbled into the bottom of my handbag, and I resolved then and there to burn that bag as soon as possible. As agreed with Jane, I then took a tram as far as Leith and handed in the Primark goods to a charity shop. I got back on the tram and made for the mall next to the Royal Yacht and headed for the coffee shop.

Jane was there before me. I told her I had it.

"Thank God for that! I think I would rather be haunted forever than renew acquaintance with Old Slimy. I got the souvenir from the tour guide pretty easily too. I think the bottom has fallen out of the ghost business; too many companies flooding the market. He ripped me off big time for the wallet though. Do you want to see it?"

She stuck her hand in her bag and pulled it out cool as ice.

"Urgh, Jane! Put it away! I don't know how you can just touch it like that! I feel like scrubbing my hand for the next millennia and I only held the book for a second."

Jane shrugged and turned the wallet over in her hands.

"Darling, I have been handling dead bodies since we were 18, this is nothing, you want to try a nice, hot, squishy brain trickling through your fingers!"

I told her to shut up or I would be sick on her Jimmi Choos.

Back in Berwick, I gave Jane a plastic lunchbox and told her to tip the two books into it and lock them in the coal shed.

"There is no way they are coming into my house. The eggcup trick might not work a second time."

"Okeydokey." She chirped grabbing both items with her bare hands, sealing them in the plastic tub and heading for the garden.

We had arranged to meet Jim at his place for dinner. He was a fabulous cook, and we had a fun night reminiscing about the old days and laughing about the ghost situation, Jane teasing me about the state of my wig and my squeamishness about the skin. We made Jim promise it was all sub-rosa. It would not do for a headmistress and a famous brain surgeon to be had up for theft of a skin-covered book, altogether too black mass and Miss Whiplash, as Jim pointed out.

Next morning, I went to mass while Jane slept off a hangover. Luckily for me, Berwick had a Polish priest owing to the large number of recent immigrants from Poland to Berwick. There was even a vigil mass on a Saturday night entirely in Polish. I hung around after the service and made sure all of the parishioners were gone before I approached him.

"Hi, Wojtek!" I called. We had met at several civic meetings, and he had been to dinner at our place a few times.

"Hi, Kate! What are you doing hanging about in that guilty manner? You haven't come to tell me you really did bump off your secretary, have you?" He laughed.

"No, I have not! Don't even joke about it. I think half of Berwick has me down as the next best thing since Lizzie Borden."

He looked at the lunchbox.

"Well, if this is going to take so long that you brought your lunch, I think we had better go back inside and sit down."

We went back into the Church and sat down on a pew near the Lady altar.

"I want you to bury what is in this lunchbox."

He looked at me puzzled, not surprising really.

"Right. Can't you bury it yourself?"

"No. I mean I want the contents to be given a decent Catholic burial. I know a requiem mass is out of the question but some sort of a service to make it rest in peace."

"Riiight…" he said.

"I know I sound like a fruitloop," I said, gingerly taking the top off the box, "but these books are covered in human skin."

Wojtek peered into the tub, and I continued.

"He was a Polish piano teacher…" I filled in the rest of the tale. I only mentioned what I knew about how he had died and what had become of his corpse.

Wojtek looked confused.

"But it was all so long ago, Kate. How did you come to hear the story and obtain these remains?"

I told him about the confession in the frame.

"I do not really want to go into how I got the remains, but these are human remains Father and I do not think it is right that they have been denied Christian burial."

Wojtek nodded.

"Of course, I agree but you know I cannot just bury them without the permission of his family. What was his last name?"

"I think it was Beretsky, Count Stanislav Beretsky. I have looked him up on Ancestors.com but cannot find any mention of him. Of course, he was a refugee, he may have used an assumed name or added a title to help him find work."

Wojtek gently lifted the box which lay between us on the pew.

"Leave him with me, Kate. I will look into his family; the Catholic Church has sources even better than Ancestors.com. I will also let the bishop know. One way or another, he will be given the respect he deserves in death that he clearly was denied in life. In the meantime, I will keep the remains behind the high altar, no one will disturb him there."

I thanked Wojtek and headed for my car. Ideally, I would have liked Wojtek to bury him in the Church garden there and then and get the whole thing done with, but big organisations grind exceeding slow and they don't come much bigger than RC PLC.

When I got back home, Jane was gone. She left a note to say that she had had an emergency call regarding a skiing accident involving a minor royal at Val d'Isere. They had sent a helicopter to my back garden to fetch her.

I had put a roast into the oven before leaving for mass and the delicious beefy aroma tempted me to make a sandwich and a cup of tea and settle down with the Sunday paper. I had just put the plate in the kitchen sink when the house phone rang.

"Hello, Berwick 2121300. How can I help you?"

It was Wojtek.

"That was quick! Have you found his relatives already?"

"No, Kate. I am not that efficient but after our conversation I decided to see if there was any mention of the Count in the Record Tenentur Parochi Persolvendi."

"The what?"

Wojtek explained that it was a secret record of the parish priests' personal impressions of the parish and parishioners. It was filled in to give any new priest a heads up so that he could hit the ground running so to speak.

"Berwick has a particularly fine, unbroken set of Record Tenentur Parochi Persolvendi dating from the foundation of the church on this site in 1829."

This was all very informative but what had any of that to do with me? I asked him.

"Well, Kate, I am not supposed to let anyone see these records, but it all happened so long ago, and you are a responsible person in the community, and I am sure you would not tell that I let you see them. In fact, you would have to swear in peril of your immortal soul that you would not…anyway, from the brief glance I have taken at them I think you should see what is written here. Can you come down now to the Church? I have to go to Alnwick for lunch with Fr Gorse. I will leave you the keys and show you where to lock the books away when you are finished. I have spare keys to the Church so just lock up and shove the keys back through the presbytery door when you are done."

I said I would come straight down and reassured him that what was read in Church stayed in Church. I put my shoes on, grabbed the car keys and set off.

Wojtek put the Record Tenentur Parochi Persolvendi for the year 1832–1833 on the pew nearest the Lady Altar and after warning me again of the trust he was placing in me, he left for lunch with Fr Gorse. For a book with such a grand title it did not look much. It was a small, green, leather-bound notebook that would have fitted neatly into a man's pocket. It was in excellent nick for its age. It had clearly never left the precincts of the vestry and been kept somewhere cool and dry. As an ex-archivist, I was used to dealing with mouse-eaten volumes kept in a loft and covered in pigeon poo so this little Victorian volume in pristine condition gave me a little professional thrill. It looked as if some eighteenth-century inhabitant had purchased it that very morning from G.C. Greaves Ltd established 1767 and still occupying the curved corner site at the bottom of Berwick Butter Market.

The leather spine creaked slightly as I opened it. I looked around, as if that would do any good, but with my recent experience of trying to read anything connected with the Count, I was apprehensive to say the least. The first page bore the book's title, the name of the parish and diocese and the year it was begun. It was written in a romantic, flowing hand; the 'f's swooping down from the top of the line to well below the next. This was lucky as I had long experience of cramped, blotchy, spidery scrawl which hurt your eyes after a bit. This handwriting was the clearest and most beautiful calligraphy I had ever seen. Had he been still alive he could have made a mint writing out wedding invitations.

The second page gave the name of the writer: Father James Andrew Bardsill and a brief history of his life and previous parishes. On page three, the fun began.

I was initially quite shocked by the frank and modern style in which Fr Bardshill laid out the pleasures and pitfalls of his first year in his new parish. He obviously had a keen eye for human foibles and failings, and I found myself smiling at the various stories of worthy matrons squabbling over positions of power and status within the parish. Alongside this were some truly heart-rending notes about the fate of the poor of the parish in the chill of winter when work was scarce and food expensive.

The year rolled on in the parish as years did then with births and marriages and deaths peaceful and sudden: crushed on the farm, lost at the fishing, taken by the smallpox. Towards the middle of 1832, there was a passing note that a Polish piano player had turned up in the parish. Fr Birdsall gave his name and the date he appeared in church for the first time and that was it.

I read on through months of routine parish business, remarking upon the appearance of the Count's name here and there. He had taken part in the Christmas Concert to raise money for the poor of the parish playing two pieces: the Bach Prelude and Fugue no.2 and Beethoven's Sonata number 8 Opus 13, commonly known as the Pathetique. This boy was clearly no slouch at the keyboard. For most of the first six months, he was in Berwick the Count clearly gave no cause for concern and seemed to be making every effort to blend in. Fr Birdsall liked him, you could tell.

The Priest began to notice, as I had, the sudden rash of deaths among the 15-year-old girls of the parish. What Fr Birdsall knew that I did not was that the Count had been employed by the parents of all of the dead girls to improve their skills on the piano. The priest had clearly been of a mind to dismiss this as coincidence. Then the Count went missing. Fr Bardshill made enquiries about his whereabouts and was told that the Count had been crushed to death on the night of 28th February by a cart when he fell into the road whilst drunk. He was also told that, as the Count had no friends to pay for his funeral, he would have been an expense upon the Council. Consequently, Mr Knox, the grain merchant and Councillor, had had his body removed to Edinburgh Anatomy School, which was run by his brother, Dr Knox. Transport of the body was paid for by Mr Knox. Fr Bardshill was furious.

I set off immediately for Councillor Knox' home on the Quay Walls. As it happens, I ran into him just outside his house. I remonstrated with him in no uncertain terms. I pointed out that the Diocese would have paid the funeral expenses for the Count so that he could have a decent Catholic burial and that he had no right to deprive the Count of the Last Rites of his Faith and the religious burial he was due as a practicing catholic.

Councillor Knox turned towards me with the look of a man who had stood at the very gates of Hell. It fairly shook me to see the difference in him. He had ever been a strutting little bantam of a man, but he stood before me truly a shadow of his former self. He then began a tale which more than explained the change in him and his actions towards the remains of the Count.

He took me into his confidence regarding a conversation he had had with his daughter, Lydia, aged 15 and also a pupil of Beretsky, in which she made certain allegations. I am sorely troubled by what Mr Knox has told me and yet I find it difficult to comprehend such behaviour towards a child. Count Beretsky had always struck me as a kind and trustworthy man, quiet and self-contained and sad at his marrow for the loss of his home and family. What the doctor has vouchsafed to me is abhorrent and so far beyond the compass of my experience that I am at a loss to know what to do. Was Count Beretsky, the sad man with the great musical gifts, really a devil with a smiling face? Surely, it cannot be and yet God himself thought Lucifer beautiful in Heaven an hour before he fell.

I sat back and said, "Wow!" I felt sandbagged. Despite the creepy events of late and the recent ghostly attempts to kill me, I had developed a warmth for the Count. I had been thinking that if someone had killed me, skinned me, turned me into book bindings and denied me benefit of sacraments for my mortal remains, I might have been inclined to be browned off and behave badly after death myself. But this, this was a whole other ballgame. Was I really being menaced and persecuted by an eighteenth-century serial killer and paedophile?

I remembered his remains were only feet away from me in their plastic lunchbox behind the high altar. The wind rattled the rafters and I nearly jumped out of my skin. I was suddenly very glad that I was on sacred ground.

Chapter 6

Next morning, I got up early and made my way to the Archives. Officially, the Archives were closed since the burst pipe incident, but I had a key to the building as I was on the Committee. I knew that the dry archival material had been removed to Morpeth and I suspected it would never return. The Council had been looking for an excuse to shift the Archive for months to cut costs, but we had fought them off up to now. The waterlogging of the precious archives had played right into their hands. No one cared about the wet letters, newspapers and diaries with their priceless information because the expense of having them professionally dried and restored was far beyond the means of the Council. It had been decided that the wet material could not be saved so after the pipe was repaired it was left to moulder away undisturbed.

As I turned the key, I remembered the advice from my tutor.

"Response to and recovery from a water disaster is most successful if collections and facilities are stabilised as soon as possible. Remove standing water, reduce and stabilise temperature and humidity, and isolate and protect dry collections. If environmental conditions are not addressed after a water problem, mould will begin to develop in as little as 72 hours, spreading rapidly thereafter. Once established, mould can be difficult to control and eradicate and may cause problems in a facility for months or even years after the recovery effort is concluded."

It had been more than 72 hours so the mould would be merrily re-producing. The only thing in my favour was another tip from my tutor.

"Do not attempt to separate soaking or very wet sheets; leave in ¼" thick stacks and separate when just damp."

The newspapers were more than ¼" thick but they had had a few days to dry out, they might be just at the right degree of moistness to separate without tearing…or they might not.

Given what had happened on my previous visit I was understandably nervous as I entered the gloomy, smelly Archives. I had little hope for any hand-written material from the 1830s as the ink was never very stable at the best of times, being made of natural dyes, it easily washed away. I had more faith that the printers' ink on the Berwick Courant might still be legible.

I pushed open the door of the room where the leak occurred. The floor was dry, there was no sound of dripping from the remaining archives but there was the whiff of damp and mould emanating from the stacks.

When I first joined the Committee, the Archive was in complete disarray. Everything was neatly wrapped and stacked but nobody had any idea where any given record was. Aided by a dedicated team, I had managed to get a filing system going. We had completed the job just before the flood. Typical! We had scrounged an old set of card filing drawers from the library which had gone digital. I walked past them now. All that work to no avail. I could see at a glance that the workmen had scooped up the soggy records and dumped them willy-nilly wherever there was a free shelf.

Luckily for me, the electricity had not been turned off. I flicked on the light. It was as cold as the grave in the damp room. Suddenly, I recalled there might be a heater left upstairs in the ex-council offices (also moved to Ashington). I tripped up the stairs and soon found an oil-filled radiator next to what had been the receptionist's desk. I lugged it downstairs and switched it on. This was the sort of low, slow-release heat that might save some of the records. I decided to leave it on when I left. If there was a fault and it burnt the place down the records would be lost, but without it they would be doomed anyway.

Luckily for me, it was easy to spot the great, green-bound tomes of the *Courant*. Even more luckily for me, the volume for 1833 was still there. I righted a table and chair from the floor and heaved the *Courant* onto the table. I sat down, took out my scalpel, in case the pages had stuck together and opened the book.

I was looking for the report on the findings of the coroner upon the death of Mrs Knox, the one who 'fell' from the widow's walk of her home on the Quay Walls. The first inch of papers were soaked and impossible to pry loose without tearing but further into the book only the edges were wet, the central body of the papers were dry and easy to read as soon as the edges were prised apart. Fortunately, the findings on Mrs Knox were published in late May, so I was able to read the following.

The Court heard from Dr Alexander Jackson who had been called to the scene of the tragic death of Mrs Eliza Knox. Dr Jackson reported that Mrs Knox was still living at the time of his arrival despite major injuries resulting from her fall from the roof. Mrs Knox said the name of her daughter, Lydia, repeatedly and then passed away in the Doctor's arms. Mr James Knox gave evidence on behalf of his daughter, a child of 15, that Mother and Daughter had been taking the air on the widow's walk above the house when a sudden gust of wind caught Mrs Knox' skirts and hurled her to the ground. The Coroner, Mr Antony Brown Q.C. reached a verdict of accidental death of both mother and unborn child, as Mrs Knox was in the early stages of pregnancy with her second child at the time of her tragic death.

Suddenly, my phone rang and my heart shot through the roof of my mouth! I scrabbled to get the phone out of my coat pocket but too late. The caller had left a message.

"Kate, it is Wojtek. I have been taking a look at the Record Tenentur Parochi Persolvendi again and I think there is something you should see. Unfortunately, I have to go on retreat to Minsteracres for a week. I will be back on the Sunday for mass. Can you see me after mass? See you then. Bye."

Chapter 7

That week, I started having accidents. It started in the street. I was shopping for Christmas wrapping paper in Berwick on a still, gloomy day when things started happening: slates flew off roofs, light fittings crashed to the ground. I gave up after the third slate and headed for home. It had been no better there before Jane came: tins flew out of cupboards, knives out of drawers and always that music, that bloody Chopin prelude! I haven't mentioned it but ever since Tom left for sea at all hours of the day and night the piano has started playing a Chopin prelude. The first couple of times I grabbed the poker and rushed into the music room ready to brain whatever intellectual burglar was invading my home. Of course, as I opened the door, the piano thrummed into silence and there was no one there. Since Jane came there had been no prelude playing and actual physical assaults with tins of beans had stopped.

Knowledge is power so they say and by this point I was feeling pretty powerless so I decided to do the only thing I knew I could do…go back to researching this whole situation to the nth degree. I picked up the car keys and headed for the drive. After what had happened lately, I was a bit iffy about getting into the car but hey, if I ended up dead that might be one way of kicking the arse of this ghostly creep: if we were all ghosts together I would make sure he got his with a cherry on the top.

The engine turned over, so far so good. I proceeded down the lane gingerly trying the brakes until I was sure they had not been tampered with by some ghastly mechanic then I turned out onto the main road and headed for the graveyard at Wallace Green.

It was another dripping grey day but this time I had taken the precaution of donning my designer wellies, the ocelot ones. I followed the track through the weeds that I had made the last time and was soon at the pink obelisk marking the last resting places of the Knox family. There was nobody about and by the look of it there had been nobody about in the intervening days.

I pulled my notebook from my pocket. Fortunately, I had had the presence of mind to note down the names of the fifteen-year-old girls who had died. I walked to the left of the Knox memorial, following the dates of death on the stones back through time.

'Alice Cameron, born 1st February 1818, died 1st February 1833. Beloved daughter of George and Muriel Cameron of Castle Hills House, Berwick upon Tweed' was not there and neither was Victoria Paxman or Georgina MacCreith.

But I did discover Margaret Ross and Isabella Watson.

The surnames of two of them rang a bell, MacCreith and Paxman. The first was the family name of Jim Scott's partner and the second was the name of a grand house not far from Berwick. Margaret Ross and Isabella Watson were the two girls who had drowned together in a boating accident.

There was also a clue about their school, Langbridge Academy, it was set in parkland on the edge of town and was still in existence today. I had met the Head several times at conferences and training days. I was sure he would allow me access to the school's archives. The school would soon be closing for the Christmas break, it was a private school and set its own term dates. I knew they had a carol service and a school show. *Joseph,* I thought, coming up, so he would be extra busy. I decided to just turn up on his doorstep. It is harder to tell people to bugger off to their face than to say so politely on the telephone or by email.

I trailed back through the wet grass and across the square to the car. I threw the wellies in the boot and tried to smarten myself up to go and meet my fellow head looking reasonably tidy. The odd request to ferret through his archives would be bad enough without looking like I was having a breakdown to boot.

The road to Langbridge took me over the Old Bridge which spans the River Tweed. The current bridge is a grade 1 listed stone structure built between 1611 and 1624. Four previous bridges stood on the site, with two destroyed by flooding: the original in 1199, and the third in 1294. The second one was demolished by an English attack in 1216 and one built in 1376, served until King James I ordered the construction of the present bridge. It was then on the main road from Edinburgh to London and the King (who was also James VI of Scotland) had had to cross over the then dilapidated wooden bridge in 1603 while travelling to London for his coronation.

From the little Old Bridge, you can see the Royal Tweed Bridge, a concrete number built in the 1920s and the Royal

Border Bridge opened by Queen Victoria in 1850. She got off her train in Berwick station and cut a ribbon then left immediately. The engineer who designed it was Robert Stevenson, son of George Stevenson. It was built for the York, Newcastle and Berwick Railway and is still in regular use today, as part of the East Coast Main Line. Despite its name, the bridge does not in fact span the border between England and Scotland, which is approximately three miles further north. It is very beautiful and has recently had all of its many arches lit at night in rainbow colours which chase each other across the Tweed.

Once across the Tweed, there is a road which curls around to a roundabout and after that a nice run along a country road between fields which brim with golden corn in the summertime. The drive up to the school cuts off to the left through an avenue of ancient trees to the front door of Langbridge Towers. I arrived there just after lunch and headed up the grand drive to the imposing portico built so that the Prince Regent wouldn't get wet when he visited for two hours on his way to Edinburgh where he donned Highland dress and looked an uber-prat poncing around Holyrood House.

I was glad of the portico though, as it had begun to snow or sleet anyway. The head's secretary showed me up to his office with the inevitable enquiry about the suicide of her opposite number.

The head's office was on the second floor, above the portico. It had a grand bow window and must have been the master bedroom when the house was a residence. The secretary rapped on the mahogany door and went straight in, she knew he was alone and could not have heard her across the vast divide from desk to door anyway.

"Dr Webster to see you, Dr Reeds."

Bill Reeds got up from behind his imposing desk and advanced across the carpet towards me.

"Kate! What a lovely surprise. Will you take tea?"

I declined the tea and Bill told his secretary that he was not to be disturbed then showed me to the settees which faced each other before an eighteenth-century marble fireplace of putti and roses. A huge fire roared in the grate. Bill was a big man, imposing, wide shoulders made even more impressive by his academic gown. Middle-aged now, he had made quite a mark in the world of rugby union. Just the ticket for a head, no child I had ever met would have been insane enough to give him cheek. He poured two whiskeys and after some chit chat about, inevitably, my suicidal secretary, I hit him with my request.

"No problem, Kate, but what on earth do you want our old records for?"

"I'm thinking of writing an article for the TES about the development of education for girls in Berwick. This was a girl's school at one point, wasn't it?"

I knew very well that it was.

"Yes, yes it was. You are a glutton for punishment Kate. I can think of better things to do with my Christmas holidays, but you are very welcome to do what you like with the records. Only thing is they are not in any kind of order. In fact, they are in the attic room above this in a load of old trunks. They are in more or less chronological order but other than that they are just thrown higgledy-piggledy into some old boarders' trunks. Do you want to see them now?"

I said that would be great if he didn't mind.

"Not in the least. Reports are all done, and I keep out of the way of all the performance carry on until I'm told to come and say how wonderful it was. I'll show you up and leave you to it while I go and speak to the caretaker about the security arrangements for the Christmas break. OK?"

He led me across the room to a staircase which ascended from the study to a hatch in the ceiling which was bolted shut.

"When this was a girl's school, the headmistress had this room as a study-come-parlour and the room above as a bedroom. This was blocked off years ago because all the heat was disappearing up the stairs."

He pulled back the bolts and pushed the hatch door until it slammed onto the floorboards of the upper room in a cloud of dust.

"Don't think I've been up here since I came to Langbridge ten years ago. There is no electricity up here but there used to be some wind-up torches on hooks just here, I think. Yes, there you go."

Bill flashed a beam of light around a small room with sloping ceilings. There was a skylight set into the ceiling but the layer of dust and the advancing dusk outside made it useless as a light source. The hatch came up in the middle of the room and at each end was a doorway with a bolt drawn across it. The floor was covered with dust and trunks and more dusty trunks. They were piled up along the edges of the room four deep and as many as six high. Someone had hastily painted the year on each trunk to indicate the age of the contents. They were not in order and piled untidily and, in some cases, upside down.

"Where do the doors go?" I asked.

Bill straightened up, wiping the dust from his hands.

"Ah, well, the old Headmistress was a strict Presbyterian and she made sure there would be no funny business going on in her school, so she insisted that all the men sleep through there and all the women slept through here." Bill indicated the two doors. "The only access to the other staff bedrooms was though her own room."

We had a joke about modern fire regs and Health and Safety requirements then Bill turned to go.

"I'll come back to close up. Good hunting!" he said as he jogged down the staircase. I heard him cross the floor of his study and close the door behind him. I was alone with the dust and the trunks and the secrets they contained.

It took me a few minutes to find the relevant year. It was upside down in the second row back, halfway along the wall. I lifted it down then dragged out a trunk from 1956 to sit on. The wind rattled the tiles above me other than that there was only the dust and the stillness and me. I put out my hand to open the lid of the trunk when a sudden brattle of hail on the roof-light made me jump. It had been a few peculiar days but I had to get a grip, I couldn't be leaping out of my skin like this every time I was on my own. I swung back the lid of the trunk. It did not creak eerily.

The contents were as jumbled as Bill had led me to believe. The Archivist in me longed to spend the next year and several hundred archive boxes getting this lot in order but for now time was pressing. Fortunately, our predecessors took clerical work very seriously and had the good sense to date all correspondence, forms etc. My torch began to dim. I grabbed it and wound it like a demon. I also took out my own from my bag in case the wind-up one suddenly went out. I was in no mood to be left alone here in the dark.

Five minutes of sifting later, I found what I had been looking for.

It was a letter from the parents of one of the drowned girls. Clearly, it was a reply to a letter of condolence sent by the Headmistress.

I had only read the first paragraph when the bolt on the door of the ladies' side of bedrooms started to rattle in its latch, probably just the wind which was getting up nicely. Distracted, I went back to reading the letter. I started at the beginning again. It was the formal greeting and thanks typical of such letters of that time when child mortality was commonplace. The rattle became more insistent. I began to think this was more than just the wind.

I was going to put down the letter, but some instinct made me shove it and the bundle it had been in, into my handbag. After the events at the Archive, I was not going to risk losing more potential clues to end all this. As I zipped my bag closed, the timbers of the door began to groan and the noise from the bolt became more and more insistent rising to a frenzied rattle. The door began shaking on its hinges, the motion joggling the bolt along ever closer to the edge of the latch.

I sprang up and dashed towards the door, running along the floorboards as the bolt slid back. I was too late.

The door burst open, and a gust of air flung into the room like a spoilt brat. It threw me backwards onto the floor the full length of the room. All the breath was knocked out of me. Gasping I got to my knees. The air was awhirl with dust and paper, struggling for breath and narrowing my eyes against the dust, I scrambled towards the precious trunk, but the lid slammed shut by itself and it rose into the air as if someone had just lifted it up. As I watched through narrowed eyes, I realised to my horror that the trunk was being tilted backwards in the air as if someone was about to beat me over the head with it. Idiot that I am, I froze.

The trunk crashed down and I would have been killed on the spot had I not been dragged to safety by, and I know this sounds ridiculous, but something else. There was no other human being there. And yet something dragged me, none too gently along the floor away from the trunk towards the opposite wall. What happened next was bizarre even by my current standards. As far as I could see through the whirling paper, a battle broke out for possession of the trunk. As it was invisibly lifted and carried towards one door, other trunks were lifted and hurled at it until it fell, only for it to be instantly lifted and pulled the other way. Trunks flew unaided back and forth banging chunks out of the plaster and the floorboards. I had to roll this way and that as I tried to make my way to the hatch dragging my bag behind me. I was nearly there when whatever it was must have realised that I had the goods in my bag then a three-way tussle broke out between the two entities, for want of a better word, and me. One of them did seem to be on my side in this but the two of us together were no match for the other one.

At this point, Bill stuck his head through the hatch. I will never forget the astonished look on his face. I tried to cry out, but I had no breath what with the struggle and the wild, whirling wind. He seemed to grasp the situation and took a grip on the bag just as a flying trunk caught me in the side and sent me sprawling along the floor. Suddenly, the wind stopped, and all the paper plummeted to the floor. The outstretched handle of my bag dropped limply. I remember thinking.

"Oh shit, this is not good!"

Bill stood in the midst of burst trunks, ankle deep in paper with plaster duster sifting down on his head. He looked bemused and was about to say something when the ominous silence was replaced by a great rushing noise gathering from the other end of the building beyond the door and hurtling towards us. Bill turned towards it. The bag handle flew out horizontally and Bill went with it. Refusing to let go, he hung full-stretch in the air. The roaring, whirling paper storm began again. I grabbed Bill's feet and pulled with all my might. He broke free and we were both knocked backwards down the hatch which slammed with a ferocious bang and what I thought was a scream of fury.

Bill shot the bolts back into place and we descended the stairs in silence. I took a seat on the couch near the fire again and Bill walked over to the sideboard.

"Drink?" he said pouring out two stiff brandies without waiting for a reply. He sat down on the facing couch and proffered me a glass. I took it and drained it in one movement. Bill took a gulp and then said, "What the hell was that all about, Kate?"

Where on earth could I begin to tell him?

"You know my secretary died?" He nodded. "Well ever since then I've been…well, haunted is the only word I can think of for it."

"By the secretary?"

"No. By the ghost of some early nineteenth century piano teacher."

Bill looked puzzled, "I think you had better start at the beginning Kate but first we had better get tidied up before someone comes in."

He was right, both of us were coated in grey dust and we looked generally dishevelled to boot, not surprising really.

Bill pointed out a door under the stairs in which was housed a small en-suite. A spare gown and a clothes brush hung behind the door. I ferreted about in my handbag and discovered an old powder compact and a lipstick. My hairstyle was beyond saving and matted with dust, so I dived into my capacious handbag again to retrieve a fur Cossack hat entirely suited to the season. I pulled it on and pushed the whisps up under the brim. Dropping the make-up back into the bag, I spotted the stolen letters and decided not to tell Bill about them.

Once Bill had donned a new gown and given his hair a thorough brush with the clothes brush, we both looked fairly normal although I could see Bill's hand shaking a bit as he raised his glass.

"The strength of that thing, Kate! What do I weigh? A good 20 stone at least and it held me in the air like a piece of gossamer. Not like any piano teacher I ever came across. How did this all begin?"

So I told him as the light dimmed beyond the great bow window and Bill flicked furtive glances at the ceiling hatch.

"That was when I noticed the pattern of deaths of fifteen-year-old girls, all of whom were at school here in 1833 so I came to check your archives for any reference to him or to their deaths."

Bill drained his second brandy.

"So you were feeding me a line about research for a TES article?"

I looked at my feet.

"Yes, but surely Bill you can see that I could not have come here this afternoon and asked to see your records because a two-hundred-year-old ghost was after me."

Bill smiled and nodded.

"Yes, I can see that. If you had I would have had to call your Chair of Governors and tell her to put on her professional psychologist's hat and pay you a visit. Have you told anyone else about this?"

"Are you nuts? The police already think I did in my secretary, what would happen if I made it common knowledge I'm being persecuted by a ghost? I'd be in Bellmarsh Hospital for the Criminally Insane."

He grinned.

"Well, look on the bright side, if they do get you for the secretary, you can plead insanity and at least get a cushy billet to serve out your time."

He offered me another drink, but I had to say no. I was on the Scottish side of the Border and Scot's law is commendably harsh on drink drivers.

"Kate, what do you think I should do about that?" He pointed to the ceiling hatch. "Should I get the vicar in or nail it up or what?"

"If I were you, I would probably do both but as you pointed out whatever else it is, it is very strong you are going to need some kick-ass vicar to get the better of it. If you take my advice, get the attic rooms blessed while the kids are off for Christmas and then nail it up. You don't want the paying customers finding out what went on up there today or any repeat performances." I picked up my gloves and fastened my coat.

Bill walked with me to the door.

"You know, Kate, I never believed in any of that afterlife stuff but as of half an hour ago, I'm a believer!"

I smiled and kissed his cheek.

"Well, some good has come out of this anyway. Merry Christmas Bill!"

I walked down the beautiful carved staircase, heaved open the massive brass furnished doors and headed for my car.

I had by now developed the habit of looking above me and all around me as I entered my own home, but the place was quiet. Not eerily quiet, just normal, which was a nice change to say the least. I trailed into the kitchen and dumped my bag on the kitchen table. The message light was flashing on the answer machine. I had missed a call from Tom. I hadn't told him about any of this because he was at sea doing a tricky and dangerous job involving explosives amongst other things, so I did my usual…pretend everything in the garden is rosy until he comes home. There was no point in demanding his return as he would have been no more use at this ghostbusting than I was myself.

I defrosted a casserole and put it in the oven to heat up while I washed the plaster and dust from my hair and soaked in a hot bath. I was just sliding into the Badedas bubbles when the bloody Chopin prelude kicked off again.

"For God's sake, give it a rest! Can't you play something else for a change?"

I yelled. Much to my surprise the piano shuddered into silence and a few moments later it set off again with Chopin's Nocturne in F major OP15. It was truly relaxing and lovely. Pain in the arse, he might be, but this ghost could play; he made Lang Lang look like a pub pianist. It was not all bad then if he was prepared to leave off hurling boarders' trunks and tins of beans long enough to take requests.

I had just finished the casserole when the phone rang. It was Jane, she was in British Colombia.

"What are you doing in British Colombia? Thought you were in France."

"I was for a few days. Turns out the minor royal had a minor bump on the head. It was nothing but they asked me to stay a few days just in case. I was forced to stay in a luxury lodge and go skiing for three days."

"So why British Colombia?"

"Lead idiot in a boy band had never been on snow in his life, decided to sniff coke and set off on a snow-board with no helmet on."

"Ouch!"

"And then some! I was on my feet for hours sorting him out, but he has come out of the coma in a lot better condition than he deserved so I am free to come home again. I am at the airport now. Back into Edinburgh tomorrow lunchtime, can you pick me up from Berwick station at 3pm?"

"Yes, of course."

"I take it your little problem is still a problem."

"And then some! I'll fill you in when you get here."

"And off she went heading for the first-class lounge and a first-class gin and tonic."

Chapter 8

I filled Jane in on the events since her departure for France. I told her about the poltergeist activity in the house and outdoors, about the trip to Langbridge Academy and all that I had found out from the archives. Then I asked her, "How come the Count is back in my house after you 'cleansed' it with the eggcups?"

"Well, we brought him back in when we brought his remains, such as they were, back to this house. Is that your famous ginger chicken in apricots I can smell?"

"Yes. I'll serve it up while you get your humpty dumptys out."

"Oh Matron!"

"Very funny. Yes, right. No cleansing no dinner. Okay?"

"Well, since he is doing requests now, should we not wait until after dinner so that we can have some lounge music provided?"

"No!"

Jane ferreted about in her capacious Coast handbag and pulled out her eggcups. She banged them together and went off to open all the windows and start clanging the little eggcups in all the corners of the house.

Over dinner, we discussed the idea that the girls who were killed had all had a schoolgirl crush on the Count and that was how he had been able to get them alone to kill them.

"Jane, remember Alf Rayburn?"

She looked up from her chicken in apricots.

"That slimy little pervert in the History department? Wasn't he given an official warning by the University to stop sleeping with the Freshers?"

"The very same. Short, dark and handsome and in a position of authority. Freshers were falling over each other to get his attention. You have to think these fifteen-year-old girls had lived very sheltered lives. The Count must have seemed like James Bond and Lancelot rolled into one for them."

"The complete bastard! It will be my total pleasure to send him on to judgement toute suite. When will his funeral take place? I only ask so that I can strap on my sparkly shoes for dancing on his grave."

****

Next day, we had a late breakfast and Jane rushed off to buy wrapping paper and cards. Ordinarily, she shopped for Christmas on Christmas Eve on the grounds that Marks and Spencer was relatively quiet by then and there was nobody about in Newcastle by about 1.30pm. The result of this was stress-free shopping for Jane and some very odd Christmas presents, as she had to gather whatever was left. One memorable year I got a selection of mustards of the world. I do not eat mustard. I have never eaten mustard.

While she was out, I retired to my study and blew the dust off some old file cards. I had not used file cards since I wrote my first dissertation in 1980, but there is something about physically moving information about that has always helped me see patterns better. I suppose, being brought up in a pre-computer age, I have an analogue brain. I had been keeping an info-diary on my laptop. I printed it off, cut it up and stuck it to the cards then started shuffling them about. There were too many gaps as yet to make any firm conclusions. Then I remembered that I had not yet examined the hard-won letters from Langbridge Academy.

I went off in search of my bag and took the letters up to my study. The bundle was about an inch thick and, much to my disappointment, contained mostly letters about late payment of fees and inquiries about fees for potential students. Not really worth having your head split open with a trunk for. There was only the one letter of interest and that was the letter from Mr and Mrs Watson thanking the Headmistress for her letter of condolence on the death of their daughter, Isabella. The paper was edged in black, and the envelope bore an X in black ink across the back. It said:

Dear Miss Crossan,

We wish to thank you for your kind words at the sad passing of our daughter. It is a consolation to us to know that she lives forever in maiden bliss with God. We have watched with sadness the loss of the other girls in her class this year and take comfort from the other parents so sadly bereft.

We thank you for the excellent education you provided for Isabella as she blossomed into an accomplished young lady.

Yours sincerely,
Maria Ross (Mrs)

'An accomplished young lady' surely meant that she played the piano. Was she another pupil of Count Beretsky? As I packed up the letters wondering whether to send them back to Langbridge or not, a newspaper cutting fluttered from the pile and settled on the carpet.

It was the report of the coroner's inquest into the death of not only Isabella Watson but also Margaret Ross.

The Court heard from PC James Tait who testified that he was called to the Quayside below the Old Bridge on the afternoon of 21 February 1833. There he discovered the bodies of Miss Isabella Watson and Miss Margaret Ross. Their remains had been dragged from the river by four fishermen using their salmon nets. The two young ladies still had their arms wound around each other in death as they had in friendship in life.

Dr Alexander Jackson gave evidence that both young ladies bore wounds about the head and face which he attributed to their being bounced along the riverbed by the current.

The last person to see the two young ladies alive was their friend, Miss Lydia Knox, who saw the young ladies walking arm in arm towards the boathouse in the grounds of Langbridge Academy on the afternoon of their disappearance. Miss Knox followed the girls but before she could catch up to them, she saw them both step into a rowboat and cast off from the shore. Miss Knox ran to admonish them but by the time she reached the riverbank the boat had been swept out to the midst of the stream. Miss Knox saw the girls stand up shouting for help and at that the boat swayed and the two young ladies were knocked into the river. Miss Knox ran back to the school to seek help but by the time she found assistance the two girls had been swept away.

Antony Brown QC stated that in his opinion both Miss Isabella Watson and Miss Margaret Ross died as a result of drowning and concluded death by misadventure. No blame was apportioned to the Academy as the boathouse was off-limits to the pupils and the rowboat, when found was in sound condition. Mr Brown thanked the fishermen and the police on behalf of the bereft parents for their delicacy and assistance.

Jane swept back in laden with the best paper and cards Berwick could offer three weeks after everyone else had picked over them. Looked like my selection of mustards might be wrapped in Bugs Bunny birthday paper again this year.

"Oh! By the way, I rang a friend of mine this morning, Diana Heggarty. She is the bee's knees when it comes to ghosts, ghouls, haunting etc. She will be here sometime in the next few days. We have to pick her up at the Station."

Great! Just what I needed another spooky old bird under my roof.

Chapter 9

Sunday rolled around again. I stuck the roast in the oven. Left Jane snoring in bed and set off for Mass. Truth to tell I couldn't wait for Mass to end so that I could get my mits on the next edition of Fr Bardshill's Record Tenentur Parochi Persolvendi. I wandered around to the back door of the church which led directly into the Sacristy. I knocked, waited and walked in when Wotjek answered…nobody wants to see a priest getting changed…psychologists' fees would be exorbitant.

"Ah, Kate! Come in. Come in."

"How was the Retreat?"

"Brilliant! I feel re-energised. What a beautiful place! Have you been there?"

"Yes. I grew up not far from there. Food's good, isn't it?"

"It is fantastic! And the monks are so funny! The chef says he is the chip monk, and his assistant is the fryer! But enough chit chat for you Kate. I can see you have come to see the Record Tenentur Parochi Persolvendi not me. Same rules as before, you have to read it here and leave it here. I marked the passage I thought you would find interesting." He pulled a more than usually festive reindeer jumper over his head. "I am going to a lunch party with the Polish Society. I can't wait!

We are having borscht and fried carp with uszka (ravioli). All rounded off with makowiec: a sort of poppy seed swiss roll and kompot which has twelve different dried fruits to represent the twelve Apostles."

He had by now donned his outdoor coat and Santa hat.

"Must dash. Just pull the door when you are done Kate. The Yale lock will be okay until I return."

With that he left tossing a scarf of tinsel over his shoulder and leaving me as keen to devour the information in the second little green book as he was to get at his makowiec. Wojtek had left a bookmark from Barter Books in the entry for 10 March 1833.

This afternoon, as I was leaving the Church grounds to visit Mr Greaves' emporium for more ink, a lady fell in a faint at my feet. I saw at once that it was Mrs Knox, the Councillor's wife. I picked her up and carried her into the Presbytery where my housekeeper, Mrs O'Neill, helped me to get her onto the settee in front of the fire in the parlour. Mrs O. applied smelling salts and the lady began to come around and I was left in charge while Mrs O. went to fetch a reviving cup of tea.

No sooner had Mrs O'Neill left the room than Mrs Knox grabbed my arm and, looking earnestly into my face said, "How could this be? It is my fault. I am her mother after all. Is it my fault? Oh, wickedness, wickedness! I allowed him liberties I should never... God forgive me. What am I to do? Now it is all too late. I have to tell the truth but what about Lydia? What will become of her if the truth is known? Yet I cannot go on with this awful lie, this terrible secret." At that point, Mrs O'Neill breezed back into the room. She clattered the teacups and Mrs Knox fairly jumped out of her skin. She barely drank a mouthful of tea and sprang up as if suddenly realising she was feasting in the tents of her enemy.

"I must go. My husband will be worried. I am quite well now. Thank you for your help."

I realised that she, a good Presbyterian, would not agree to be seen with a Priest on the streets of Berwick so I offered the services of Mrs O'Neill to walk her home. She accepted and I was glad because in truth she was still unsteady on her feet.

When Mrs O'Neill returned, she came in to see me in such a rush that she was still undoing the strings of her bonnet.

"There now," she said, "wasn't I only saying to Mrs O'Brien yesterday that there was something fishy going on in that house. Who waits fifteen years between babies unless it is a case of a second husband? I know for a fact that Mr and Mrs Knox have separate rooms, I got it from Mary Jenkins' girl Annie who is parlour maid there. The only time they shared a bed was when his brother and her parents came for Christmas just gone. I heard every word through the door Father, if that is not a guilty conscience, I never heard one!"

I admonished Mrs O'Neill most severely and swore her to secrecy on pain of her immortal soul. I had no idea that Mrs Knox was with child. No wonder Councillor Knox looked such a worried man when I saw him that day on the Quay Walls. I have written down verbatim what Mrs Knox said and rereading it I am still unsure what she meant. Is Mrs O'Neill right to imply that the Count fathered her child? Was her concern for Lydia that her reputation would be ruined by proxy if it became known that her mother had lain with the piano tutor? Neither Mrs O'Neil nor I will ever speak of this again but clearly all is not well in the house on the Quay Walls.

Talk about hot stuff! I have always known that people are people and sticking them in bonnets and tailcoats does not alter basic human nature. I recall reading letters in cuneiform on clay tablets from Ur where a lad was frantic because he got the neighbour's daughter in the family way. Clearly, this pianist was after anything with a pulse.

It all made me think again about Mrs Knox' mysterious death. Was she blown from the roof, or did she jump because of the disgrace? Poor Lydia, in the first few months of 1833 she had been molested by a paedophile, lost five schoolfriends, the drowning of two of whom she actually witnessed, and now it looked like she had been too late when she rushed up to the roof to prevent her own mother from topping herself.

Suddenly, I remembered that the remains of the Count were lying just the other side of the wall I was sitting beside. Had I done the right thing in arranging for him to have a proper burial? Didn't he deserve to spend forever as an exhibit being gawked at? The ruin he had wreaked upon the children and families of Berwick-upon-Tweed. Still, properly committed, he would stand before the Throne of Judgement. As soon as Wojtek got the all-clear from the bishop, the Count was going down.

I copied the relevant section from the Record, as I had the last time and I headed for the door. I pulled the door shut and checked it with my hip then, pulling on my fur hat against the chilly mist, I began the slog up the hill to home.

****

My kitchen table was covered in Sellotape, scissors, glitter pens, ribbon and inappropriate wrapping paper. On the back of an over-priced Christmas card, Jane had left a note to say that she had caught the only train to Aberdeen. As well as patting the hands of boy band idiots and Saudi Royals for her weight in gold, Jane did her thing gratis for the NHS. Apparently, a little girl in Aberdeen had slipped on some ice and fallen badly, a tricky blood clot needed Jane's attention. I made a roast beef sandwich rather than dinner again, as there was only me to eat it, and retreated to my study. It was kind of odd to feel that the oddness had gone from the house.

I copied the notes from the record onto file cards and added them to the existing pile. Evidence against the Count was circumstantial but pretty overwhelming. I read through the file cards again and decided I might as well try to get my hands on the Coroner's Reports for the remaining girls: Georgina MacCreith, Margaret Ross, Isabella Watson and Lydia Knox. I checked the National Archives website. It had the following advice:

The majority of post mid-eighteenth century records of inquests are held at local archives and not The National Archives. Not all coroners' inquests have been selected for permanent preservation. Records of deaths less than 75 years old may be retained by the coroner's office. From the nineteenth century onwards, a newspaper report may be the only surviving account. Locate newspapers held at local libraries or the British Library Newspaper

Collections which may provide details of an unexpected, sudden or suspicious death.

Well great! "From the nineteenth century onwards, a newspaper report may be the only surviving account." Well, thank you very much Count Beretsky for throwing what may have been the only record of the Reports on the deaths of these girls into two feet of rusty water. I knew for a fact that Berwick local library did not have copies of old newspapers because, ironically, I was the one who physically carried them out of the damp library cellars into the 'dry, safe storage' at the Archives. As for the British Library Newspaper Collections, they would charge an absolute fortune to send copies to Berwick.

I had a brainwave. I typed the name of the current Berwick Newspaper, *The Berwick Gazette* into a search engine. *The Berwick Gazette* had been on sale in Berwick since 1808 and in 1850 the owner, Colonel Jabez Small, had bought out *The Berwick Courant* to reduce competition. That meant it was just possible that *The Berwick Gazette* had kept the old copies of *The Berwick Courant* which it gained as part of the deal. First thing next morning, I would visit the offices of *The Berwick Gazette* and investigate.

Chapter 10

Mrs Diana Heggarty stepped down from the train onto Berwick Station Platform 2.

She was a tall woman of Valkyrie build. She wore brown leather sandals on her bare feet, navy palazzo trousers with elasticated waist, a white georgette, sleeveless top and an over blouse to match. A young man heaved her huge four wheeled case down the steps behind her. As soon as her feet touched the ground, I felt that a definite presence had arrived. Her bust alone could have flattened the front row of a battalion of Coldstream guards, if any human being was going to kick the Count out of town, my money was on her. According to Jane, Diana was pushing seventy, but I never would have thought it. There were a few smile wrinkles around her eyes but other than that her skin was supple and peachy. She had twinkly hazel eyes and gave off what Jane would call an 'aura' of capable, unflappable, rosy cheeriness. Jane hugged her and introduced me. "Call me Diana," she said. "Ah! You have hazel eyes like me, another earth witch, Jane!"

Jane looked a bit embarrassed. I knew her as a medical student, a doctor, a consultant, a lecturer. Of course, I knew she did her supernatural thing but she never talked about her colleagues/co-workers/co-witches or whatever. What on earth was I doing with these people? But then what option did I have?

Jane had told me that Diana loved a good curry, so after dumping her gear at my place, we headed for the Gate of India which did a delicious lunchtime special. As soon as the order was placed and our drinks had arrived, Diana got straight to the matter in hand.

"Start from the beginning. First of all, tell me what he looks like."

I knew that Jane had sent Diana a full and accurate account of all that had happened because she had me proof-read it to check she hadn't missed anything. At no point had I told anyone that I had seen him because I hadn't.

"I never saw him, Diana. I felt his hand upon my left shoulder." Unconsciously, I put my hand up to the place. "But I never saw him as such."

Diana smiled at Jane as if a baby had just said something cute and adorable.

"Kate, you know what he looks like. You have known from that instant. He is haunting you darling. As that poor woman told you in her suicide note, he has chosen you, whether you like it or not, the two of you are linked until the link is broken. Now let's start with you giving me an idea of how tall he is say."

She had leaned towards me, and I could see the golden flecks in her hazel eyes, they seemed to have a gleam about them, mesmerising. I opened my mouth.

"He is about six feet tall, same as my Tom, bigger build though across the shoulders, dark blonde hair, dark eyes. I can feel his hand still upon my shoulder, heavy, not with pressure but with the weight of the bones. Tom's hand is like that too from decades of playing the piano."

Where did that come from? I had known that. Since when had I known that?

Diana leaned forward and patted my hand.

"It comes under unknown knowns, darling. Now what impression did you have when he touched you?"

I blushed, I could feel it, so long since I blushed, I had almost forgotten the feeling.

"Come on now, darling, Jane and I are unshockable!"

I could not believe what I was about to say.

"I felt thrilled and giddy and terrified all at once. Like riding a ghost train with your first boyfriend."

Was this rubbish really coming out of my mouth?

"Hmm," said Diana and Jane looked worried.

When we got back home, I went indoors to make a cup of tea while Jane and Diana strolled around the garden. I could see them from the kitchen window deep in conversation. Jane seemed to be upset about something and arguing her case while Diana, unperturbed, gave short, calm replies. Eventually, Jane seemed to give up and accept the inevitable, whatever that was. They had reached the summer house and sat down on the veranda, Diana lifting her face to the winter sun. I made the tea and took it out to the garden.

"So, what is the plan then?"

Diana looked at Jane and Jane said, "We do have a plan, Kate, but we cannot tell you what it is."

This was a bit rich when I was the one, as Diana herself had pointed out, who was being haunted.

"Why not? Does it involve some top-secret, witches-only claptrap? Not accessible to the uninitiated?"

Diana gave me the tolerant smile again.

"No, darling, you are by way of being a security risk."

I stopped mid-pour, the teapot in mid-air.

"What?"

"What you know he knows. I told you about the link, it works both ways you see. We don't want to telegraph our moves before we make them."

I smacked the teapot down on the table.

"That is ridiculous. How am I supposed to be telling somebody, a somebody who is, if I may remind you, dead, anything at all?"

Jane put her oar in at this point.

"By choosing you, Kate, he opened a door, and he is standing there listening to everything you say and do. He has been all along and I'm afraid that may not be the worst of it."

I had the urge to tell the pair of them to clear off and never come back.

"Oh really? Well spit it out then, what fresh Hell is coming my way?"

Diana took up the reins.

"You remember the police told you that they suspected Gillian was pushed under the train?"

I didn't like the way this conversation was going but she continued, "Well, we have to face it darling…it may have been you."

I couldn't believe my ears.

"Oh, fine, right, well I suppose I set fire to Jim's office and flooded the archives as well!"

"Precisely."

I was speechless, Jane took my hand.

"Look, we are not saying you did this when you were in your right mind."

"Oh, great! So now I'm crazy as well as a murderer, arsonist and vandal. Well, that's all right then!"

Neither of them said anything. I tried to get my head around it.

"So, what you are saying is… I have been used like a glove puppet. The Count has stepped into my body like a pair of second-hand shoes and walked about in it."

Diana sipped her tea.

"That's a possibility. Yes." Diana closed her eyes and turned her face to the sun again. "More tea and Hobknobs wouldn't come amiss."

I looked down at the tray. All the biscuits were gone. I wondered momentarily if I had eaten them all and not realised until I saw Diana brushing crumbs off the shelf that was her bosom. Jane picked up the tray and followed me back to the house. She stacked the cups in the dishwasher and unhooked new mugs from the dresser while I filled the kettle.

"Cheer up, Kate. It isn't as bad as it seems."

I turned to face her.

"How is that, Jane? You heard what she said. I threw Gillian under a train! I never liked the woman, but I never, ever considered throwing her under a train! It is all my fault."

"No, it isn't."

"Please Jane don't give me all that crap about not being myself at the time. These hands did the deed Jane, my hands. Not to mention nearly killing Jim Scott."

I sat down in a lump on the kitchen chair.

"It is a possibility, yes, but only a possibility. I know you better than Diana does. I don't think the most powerful spirit in the world could overcome the spirit you possess yourself. I've certainly never won an argument with you and God knows I've tried. You are not some wishy-washy teenager that any passing wraith can move into at will."

I looked up hoping against hope she was right.

"And as for Jim Scott, well please! Don't you remember him at university? He smoked everything he could get his hands on: tobacco, weed, old coir doormats. He's got lungs like a carthorse. He is absolutely fine, and the insurance are paying up for a total office refurb so believe me he is a happy boy. Lighten up, for God's sake!"

I tried a smile.

"But what if Diana is right and I go after her or you or A.N. Other?"

"No chance of that we will have you under around the clock surveillance just in case."

I laughed.

"I'm serious," she said. "You must realise Kate that given what happened to Gillian the real danger now is to one person only."

I suddenly realised she meant me.

Chapter 11

Next morning, Jim Scott rang.

"I've got some excellent news for you Petal. Come down to the office right away!"

Any excuse to get away from Jane and more so Diana who had taken to wafting me with burning sage smoke at every opportunity. I headed for Jim's office. When I got there the air was filled with the whine of power tools as assorted workmen got to grips with the office refurbishment.

"Let's go next door for a coffee," Jim yelled above the din.

We ordered coffee and sat down in a quiet corner at the back of the coffee shop.

"So?" I said. "What is the good news? Have the National Trust agreed to take on the house?"

"Make a decision at Christmastime? You must be joking! No. Anyway it is better news than that!"

The waitress brought the coffees and left.

"Come on then? Don't keep me in suspense. Believe me my nerves are in no fit state."

Jim pulled an iPad out of his briefcase tapped it a few times and handed it to me. There was a video clip of Berwick Station on pause.

"Run the video. There is no CCTV at Berwick Station, but DC Kirsty did not reckon on some sad git of a train-spotter videoing the trains from the bridge. Look!"

I looked. There was the Inverness express hurtling towards Berwick Station. The angle of sight was from the bridge, but you could see Gillian clearly. She was standing alone on the edge of the platform. It looked as though she was arguing with someone, but there was nobody else there. As the train approached, she suddenly flew backwards as if some invisible force had pushed her really hard. Jim pressed pause.

A wave of relief washed over me.

"There is more of it, but you do not want to see it, trust me. Apparently, it has gone viral in the snuff movie world, and it is causing quite a stir in the alien/supernatural nut-job fraternity."

"What about the Police? They need to see this."

Jim closed the iPad and put it away.

"They have seen it. DC Cameron seemed really disappointed and still quite keen to finger you for the death, but wiser heads prevailed."

"The little cow!"

"That was certainly my impression. I think she has teacher issues; some perceived slight from the past and she has made it her mission to get the lot of you and the horse you rode in on. Meanwhile, the Police are going with the theory that the train created some kind of a vortex which sucked her off the platform. Anyhoo, this all means that there will be no challenge regarding your right to own and therefore, sell the house. While they had suspicions that you had bumped her off you could not have benefitted from her will, but as things now stand you are free to get rid of it."

I had not changed my mind on that score.

"I have not changed my mind about that. I want to give it away to the National Trust; I told you that."

Jim shook his head.

"I think you are crazy, but if you persist in this, I have to do it. I will open negotiations as soon as I actually have the deeds in my hands."

"What! I thought you sent for them already."

"It may have escaped your notice darling, but I have been a touch pre-occupied, what with being almost barbequed and having my office burnt out etc. Anyway, the usual waiting time for the Registry is about four weeks though with this being Christmas... In addition, there may be some issues about selling or even giving away a house that is known to be haunted. Whilst there is no statute that requires a seller to pro-actively disclose the existence of paranormal activity in a house to a buyer and anyone then encumbered with a house they consider uninhabitable due to spectral activity, this offence does not render the contract void or unenforceable, nor does it provide them with a right of action in civil proceedings with regards to any loss that arises as a result of an offence under the provision. The most relevant statute is the Property Misdescriptions Act 1991. This Act provides that it is an offence to make a false or misleading statement, which may occur either in writing or verbally, in the course of selling a house. This does not place a duty on you to pro-actively disclose that a house is rumoured to be haunted, it simply provides that if asked, and the seller is aware of the fact, you cannot lie without committing an offence. The penalty for the offence is a fine."

"Thank you, Perry Mason."

"Well, I am just carrying out my duty as your legal advisor to inform you of all the relevant facts."

"So, the relevant facts are: there is no way I can off-load this house before Christmas and there is the possibility that I will never off-load it because it is widely known, even to serving police officers, to be, in fact, haunted."

"That's about the size of it, but let's face it some people might like the fact that it is spooked. There are some weirdos out there, I should know in my game. The National Trust may even take it as an added incentive, they could run paranormal weekends and rake in the cash."

I sighed. "Just get a move on and get rid Jim."

It was then I remembered I wanted a favour.

"Jim, do you know who manages PaxmanTrust these days?"

He looked puzzled.

"Yes, it's Ian Sinclair of Sinclair and Brown why?"

"Would you ask him if I could have a rummage through their archives? I know they keep them in the attic rooms because I tried to get them brought into the Archives, but he would not have it."

Jim smiled.

"Just as well under the circumstances!"

"Oh, ha, ha! Would you just ask him?"

"No bother."

We chatted about his office renovations and our plans for Christmas, but my mind was really not concentrating. I couldn't wait to get back home to tell Jane and Diana. No ghost was moving into my bodily premises, not then, not now, not ever.

I stormed into my kitchen ready to go. "Ner-nerny-ner-ner I told you so!" Only to find another of Jane's notes. She had been called away again and Diana had headed off to Witchy HQ to research their library for useful methods for getting rid of unwanted guests.

I felt decidedly flat and at a bit of a loose end. Then I remembered the archives of the Berwick Gazette. I scooped up my bag, pulled on my hat and set off into to the light drizzle to walk to the Gazette Offices at the top of Berwick Marketplace.

The Berwick Gazette Building is a detached, imposing, three storey, stone edifice next door to a shoe shop. It has the words Berwick Gazette emblazoned across its frontage in two feet high white letters. The glazed, Victorian door is set to the left. I turned its brass handle and went in. The front office was recently done up, that is to say, around about 1930. It has a bottle green linoleum floor in front of a grained wood and figured glass partition. There is a bell on the counter. I pressed it and the partition slid back.

"Oh hello, Dr Webster! How are you?" said Mrs Renfrew, mother of Daisy (Year 1) and Phoebe (Year 3). "Isn't it awful about poor Mrs Morris?"

This was a bit rich coming from the woman who had recently exploded into my office screaming, "If that bitch upsets my bairns again, I'll kick her bloody teeth in!" However, this was the perfect opportunity to start redressing the balance.

"Yes. We were all devastated about the accident."

She looked like one who was not going to have the wool pulled over her eyes by the likes of me.

"Accident? Was it?"

"Oh yes, haven't you seen the video?"

I pulled my iPad out of my bag and showed her the snuff video I had downloaded for the purpose…minus the gory bits of course.

She looked bitterly disappointed.

"I'm so pleased. It must have been awful for you, having the suspicion hanging over your head like that." A brief pause… "Of course, I never believed it for a moment."

I smiled benignly.

"Thank you, Mrs Renfrew. Now, would it be possible to have a look at the newspaper archives do you think?"

She looked worried. Obviously, word had gotten around about what happened the last time I was let loose with anything old and dusty.

"Yes, of course…but I will have to be in the room with you…nothing personal you know, just company policy. Which year would you like?"

Five minutes later, I was sitting in a room on the first floor overlooking the marketplace with a single volume of the Berwick Courant for 1833 resting on a green leather covered desk. I took out my pad and pen and cracked open the volume which had clearly never been read before. It was in pristine condition. I skimmed through to March and began to scan the deaths columns looking for the remaining girls.

The first one I came across was Alice Cameron who had passed away on her fifteenth birthday. It was the usual death notice giving her birth and death dates, the names of her parents and a text from the Bible. Isaiah 40:11 "He tends his flock like a shepherd: He gathers the lambs in his arms and carries them close to his heart." Which I thought was rather lovely.

Instead of looking for the death notices of the others I flicked through the papers until I found the coroner's report on Alice's death. By this time, Mrs Renfrew had given up sighing, shuffling and tutting and decided to abandon the records to their fate and leave me to it. I could hear her annoying whine telling everyone who entered the office the tale of the train vortex and the snuff movie.

The court heard from Dr Alexander Jackson who had been called to the scene of the tragic death of Miss Alice Cameron. Dr Jackson reported that Miss Alice Cameron was still living at the time of his arrival despite major injuries resulting from the fire. She was unable to speak and within minutes lapsed into a coma for several hours after which, despite his ministrations, the young lady passed away. Mr Robert Cameron gave evidence that his daughter, a child of 15, had been enjoying her birthday party with her friends. They had a party tea and as a special treat Miss Cameron's piano teacher, Count Stanislav Beretsky had attended the soiree to play a little waltz written especially for the occasion. As the party was drawing to its close the girls went upstairs to retrieve their cloaks from Miss Cameron's bedroom. It was at this time that Miss Cameron must have lost her footing and sadly, her dress billowed out towards the fire. Miss Cameron's party dress was made of a pink tissue which was instantly ablaze. Some of the young ladies ran for help whilst others utilised pillows to beat out the flames.

The coroner, Mr Antony Brown Q.C. commended the actions of the young ladies: Misses Georgina MacCreith, Margaret Ross, Victoria Paxman, Lydia Knox and Isabella Watson before reaching a verdict of accidental death.

Poor girl. What an awful death for anyone, let alone a young woman on her birthday. It made it so much worse to think that only minutes before she had been so happy with her pink party dress, her friends around her and a waltz written especially for her birthday. Well, at least this death could not be laid at the Count's door. He would not have been allowed into a young lady's bedroom and it was clear that there were several witnesses to what was obviously a terrible accident.

Outside the window, the light was starting to dim and large cumuli nimbus clouds were gathering over the farmland on the other side of the river. I closed the volume and packed away my notes then headed for home.

Back in my kitchen I noticed the red light flashing to indicate I had a message waiting. It was from Wojtek.

"Hi, Kate. You must come and see me at once. I have such exciting news about the Count!"

He sounded excited on the phone and went into transports when I rang him back, though he would not tell me anything until we met face to face. I arranged to see him at the Presbytery at 6pm and went off to heat up some home-made soup I had left over from the day before.

When I rang the Presbytery bell at 6pm on the dot, the door flew open, and Wojtek yanked me indoors.

"What's all the rush? He's been dead nearly three hundred years, whatever you've found out can't be all that important."

Wojtek was practically leaping from foot to foot with excitement.

"But it is, Kate! It really is!"

He remembered his manners and offered me tea which I accepted, and he called for his elderly housekeeper to fetch it. He refused to say a word about the Count until after she had gone and then he flung open the door to be sure she was not listening. She wasn't. Being deaf as a post, it would have done her no good either way.

"Come on, Wojtek! Enough of the drama. I take it you have found something out about the count?"

"No, Kate. I have found out everything about the count!"

He then began at the beginning and continued on through a very long, detailed and confusing tale about the Count's involvement in a very important conflict between Poland and Russia. I have summarised it in as much as I understood it, given the fact that Wojtek was so excited that he occasionally lapsed into Polish for parts of the story.

It appears that Stanislav Beretsky was born on March 16, 1805, in the manor house of the Beretsky family in Warsaw, Poland. He was the eldest son of Marianna and Józef Beretsky, who was one of the town's most notable inhabitants. His family bore the Ślepowron coat of arms. The Beretsky family was Roman Catholic and early in his youth, Sanislav Beretsky attended an elite college run by Theatines, a male religious order of the Catholic Church in Warsaw, and finished his education there before attending Warsaw Officers' School. Wojtek also had a copy of a miniature of the Count. He was dressed in a military uniform; navy blue with a gold velvet collar and epaulettes, on his white stock a medal was pinned, it was in the shape of a Maltese cross with a golden eagle falling from it. The Count looked familiar, one of Diana's unknown knowns.

"I have his final report from the Theatines. Look, Kate, he was a brilliant student and played the piano to a professional standard. They say that he was kind, honest and hard-working."

Wojtek went on. The November Uprising (1830–1831), also known as the Polish-Russian War 1830–1831 or the Cadet Revolution, was an armed rebellion in the heartland of partitioned Poland against the Russian Empire. The uprising began on 29 November 1830 in Warsaw when the young Polish officers from the local Army of the Congress, Poland's military academy, revolted, led by lieutenant Piotr Wysocki, a young cadet from the Warsaw Officers' School.

Piotr Wysocki, took arms from their garrison on 29 November 1830 and attacked the Belweder Palace, the main seat of the Grand Duke. The final spark that ignited Warsaw was a Russian plan to use the Polish Army to suppress France's July Revolution and the Belgian Revolution, in clear violation of the Polish constitution. The rebels managed to enter the Belweder Palace, but Grand Duke Constantine had escaped in women's clothing. The rebels then turned to the main city arsenal, capturing it after a brief struggle. The following day armed Polish civilians forced the Russian troops to withdraw north of Warsaw. This incident is sometimes called the Warsaw Uprising or the November Night or in Polish Noc listopadowa.

"Noc listopadowa, Kate! Noc listopadowa! The remains of a Polish hero, a friend of Piotr Wysocki, are lying in an ice cream box behind my altar!"

"This is important then?"

"Important? Yes, Kate! This is mega-important. After the end of the November Uprising, Polish women wore black ribands and jewellery as a symbol of mourning for their lost homeland. The Scottish poet Thomas Campbell wrote *The Pleasures of Hope*, about it and he said, 'Poland preys on my heart night and day'. Edgar Allan Poe volunteered to fight the

Russians during the November Uprising. Honestly Kate, if there were no Brits involved you know nothing about history!"

Fair comment, but I felt I had had the full nineteenth century course that night.

"Oh, good heavens Kate. I shall have to tell the Polish Ambassador and there will be representatives of the Ślepowron families and of course the Count's own relatives. Berwick will never have seen a funeral like this!"

I felt bad at having to burst his bubble.

"Wojtek, don't you think the fact that all we have of him is a few scraps of skin still wound around a couple of jotters might cause his relatives to question our treatment of their hero? I can see this blowing up into a major international incident."

I had burst his bubble well and truly.

"I had not thought of that. But Kate, he is a National hero, I cannot just throw him into a wet hole and leave him there."

"No, of course, but perhaps something low key. After all, Wojtek, we are not, as yet able to prove that he did not have anything to do with the girls' deaths or Mrs Knox' baby and suicide. Did you find out anything about how he came to be in Berwick?"

"Kate, I cannot believe that a hero of Noc listopadowa was the villain that you paint him!"

"I am not trying to paint him as a villain. I am trying to get to the bottom of a very old mystery. Keep in mind it was I who rescued his remains and brought them to you for burial. I could have left them where they were or dug a wet hole in my garden and thrown them in." Although even saying such a thing made me feel queasy beyond belief.

"You are right, Kate. I just got carried away. I am sorry. I know your heart is in the right place. You asked me how he came here. Well, there was an Association of the Friends of Poland set up in London. When the Polish army surrendered in Brodnica on the Prussian border, the Association helped some of the officers to purchase passage to England and he was lucky enough to be one of those helped. He boarded a ship heading back to Berwick. You know all there is to be known after that from the Record Tenentur Parochi Persolvendi."

Despite my best efforts to persuade him, Wojtek refused to just bury the remains quietly with just the two of us there.

"You do not get it, Kate. This man was so important in the history of my country. Would you ask a Scotsman to bury Robert the Bruce in an ice cream box? No. You must get to the bottom of your mystery Kate and clear his name. Then he can receive the respectful burial he deserves and has been denied for so long. Incidentally, Kate, how did you come to know about the Count's remains and the mystery in the first place?"

I was baptised the day that I was born. Not officially, that came three weeks later, but my granny was taking no chances and doused me in the name of the Lord, claiming me for the Catholic Church as soon as she got her hands on me. She didn't want me to wait in Purgatory with the Holy Innocents until the end of time in case I died with the stain of Original Sin upon me.

There are two things no Catholic would ever be comfortable doing:

1. Lying to their priest.
2. Letting their priest know they had been in communication with dead people.

I decided to go for obfuscation.

"I was working in the Berwick Archives when I found out most of it. Initially, it was something my secretary put me on to… God rest her soul."

The conversation turned to the odd circumstances of Gillian's death. I showed Wojtek the edited snuff video. He blessed himself and said he would say a mass for the repose of her soul. Gillian was not a Catholic but what with bumping off her husband and all, she was probably happy at this point to take all the help she could get.

I walked back through the gloom of a winter's night. The town was foggily quiet, every footstep deadened and not a car or a soul in sight. Beads of moisture pearled on my fur hat and chilly damp seeped into the marrow of my bones. I was looking forward to round two with the homemade soup, so I picked up the pace and was soon stomping through my kitchen door. Only to find Jane sitting at my kitchen table polishing off the last of the soup.

"Hi, Kate! Sorry about the disappearing act."

"What was it this time? Another skiing accident for the grand Pooh-bah of Tittyfallah?"

"No. A builder in Carlisle had fallen off a frosty scaffold. A piece of bone was where it shouldn't be, just a quickie really. So, here I am again. What's new?"

I told her whilst scrounging about for something edible.

"If you are scrounging about for something edible forget it, Diana has gone to that curry house for a slap-up dinner. I'm surprised you did not run into her on the way back from Wojtek's."

Well, that rounded off a perfect day. All I needed was Jane's dippy pal!

"I know you think she is dippy, but she is a lot smarter than she looks. When the shit really hits the fan over this, you will be damned glad she's here."

"I thought she had gone to Witchy HQ in Glastonebury or Tintagel or wherever you people hang out when the moon is full."

"First of all, less of the 'you people' and second of all Witchy HQ as you put it is in Hexham."

"Hexham!"

"Yes. Clue's in the name dimwit. Hex meaning witch or possibly spell and ham meaning town."

"Well, I never. Fancy that. I was born only minutes from Hexham as the crow flies, and it never occurred to me what the name meant."

At that point, Diana breezed in like a small typhoon and heaved a huge bag of delicious Indian treats onto the table. All this while, Jane had had the plates warming in the Aga…a miraculous event in its own right…and soon the kitchen was filled with the fumes of red wine, cumin, and all the spices of Arabie.

Diana proved to be an excellent dinner companion, not at all the mad bitch I had originally thought her to be. She had been one of the youngest female Police Inspectors ever in the country and had lectured in computing at Hendon Police College until arthritis had cut her down in her prime. The tales she could tell had us crying with laughter. When Jane volunteered to wash up…another miracle! Diana leaned towards me over the table and said, "Did you know only five percent of all of the people in the world have hazel eyes?"

I did in fact know that. My dad always used to say to me, "If you are ever hung for good looks, you'll die innocent!" Fair comment actually, but people have always complimented me on my eyes.

"See my eyes are the same colour as yours."

I looked into Diana's hazel eyes and as I looked the golden flecks in them seemed to gleam like 24 carat gold. I started to feel warm and woozy, happy and floaty.

"Did Jane say you had Welsh blood in your family?"

"Yes. My Nain was from Pontycymer. She didn't speak English until she was eight years old."

"Did she teach you any Welsh?"

"Yes, she taught me the rhyme of Three Little Kittens but I think I must have remembered it wrong because when I say it for Welsh speakers, they do not understand it. She was going to teach me to speak Welsh, but she died suddenly before we got any further than Three Little Kittens."

"I don't think I ever heard any Welsh spoken. Will you say it for me?"

Odd request but I set off chanting it the way my Nain taught me.

Jane turned around from the sink and froze with a plate in mid-air. Diana smiled, then suddenly leaned forward and touched me on my forehead pulling her fingers briskly away.

"That's better. You'll be able to see properly now."

So, saying she got up and headed for the stairs.

"Goodnight, darlings!"

I swung around to Jane.

"What did she do? What did she mean I'll see better? There's nothing wrong with my eyesight!"

Jane sat down and put on her earnest face. This was always bad; I had seen it the time she borrowed my brand new car and crashed it. I had seen it when she was larking about with my mother's Venetian glass galleon and smashed it.

"Oh shit, Jane! What did she do?"

"Look, calm down. All she did was open your chakra, your third eye so to speak."

"I thought a third eye was a cat's backside and that seems to be what you are talking out of Jane!"

"Will you calm down? All she has done is free your natural powers. They were in there all along and you know it. It is just all those years of brainwashing by God's Stormtroopers that stops you admitting it."

"They were Dominican nuns, Jane, not Jedi from the Dark Side!"

"I know very little History, Kate, but I am almost sure the Dominicans ran the Spanish Inquisition. Look Kate, it is your destiny, your birth rite. You come from a long line of Welsh witches; you told me that yourself."

"It was a joke, Jane! Just something we used to say in the family whenever somebody had déjà vu."

"Well, I don't think it was a joke Kate because your Three Little Kittens is not a rhyme. It is a spell. A protection spell your Nain gave you to keep you safe. Do you or do you not say it in your head when the going gets tough?"

I had said it over and over in my head ever since DC Kirsty Cameron had first poked her pretty, little head through my office door. I didn't reply.

"See? You told me yourself about your Nain seeing her father's ghost with a warning the day her husband died. What about you playing on the stairs with Elizabeth's ghost when you were tiny and the prophetic dreams you have had that always come true?"

Why had I told her this? She was using my own family history against me. It was true that my Nain received the warning from her dead father. She was ascending the stairs holding a pile of ironing when she saw him coming down. He stopped and said, "It'll be all right, Ruth, you'll survive this." Then he continued on down the stairs and disappeared. Minutes later, men were knocking at the back door to say her husband had been killed in the pit. It was also true that every little girl in our family, me included, had played with Elizabeth on the stairs. Technically, Elizabeth was my aunt. She had died tragically aged three years when she tripped and hit her temple on the edge of the fireplace. It was also true that certain types of dream I had always came true.

"Oh my God! I'll never be normal again!"

"Since when were you normal? I hate to point this out blossom but the activity you have experienced in the last few days would have somebody normal in a monastery or a mental home by now. You have just kept calm and carried on because you have been aware of things all your life and just refused to admit it. It is as natural to you as it is to me."

"Just tell me one thing, Jane. Does this mean I'll be like you now? I'll see dead people at every turn?"

"No. It just means you can see them and hear them come to that, if you want to and only if you want to. You can close your third eye just like your physical eyes. However, it will come in handy when tackling whatever is causing all this trouble."

All this trouble. It suddenly occurred to me that there had been no trouble whatsoever for days. I had researched archives without having to fight ghostly forces. I had consulted Jim Scott about the house without having to call for the fire brigade. It suddenly dawned on me that it was over! Maybe all Beretsky wanted was to have his remains properly put to rest. It was all over. I said as much to Jane.

"Of course, it is not over! It has barely begun!"

I pointed out my evidence that there had been no poltergeist activity of any kind for a week.

"I should bloody well hope not! Diana has been knocking herself out on your behalf to protect you from it!"

"I wouldn't call wafting sage smoke over me with an eagle feather every five minutes 'knocking herself out'. I don't see what else she has done other than hoover up every Hobknob in the place."

Jane looked furious.

"Look behind that curtain."

I looked. To my horror I saw that Diana had drawn a pentangle in a circle near the window frame.

"Bloody hell fire, Jane! That wallpaper is Heritage range! It was £60 a roll!"

Jane clearly did not appreciate the seriousness of somebody doodling on my expensive wallpaper.

"I'll have you know that doodling as you call it would cost you megabucks if Diana were not a friend of mine. Those doodles…"

"What there are more!"

I looked behind the curtain on the other side of the window and sure enough there was another one.

"Of course, there are more! They are now each side of every window and door in the house that is what is keeping the evil out. As I was saying, those doodles are apotropaic symbols also known as witch marks. Apotropaic comes from the Greek word for averting evil and they are not pentangles they are hexafoils also known as daisy wheels. In addition to that, Diana has salted the entire outer and inner perimeter of your property. She has used a real Tibetan singing bowl to properly cleanse the place from attic to cellar and if you think it was easy getting a woman that size up your loft ladders you can think again. She has installed a water feature in your garden to purify the environment. She has scrubbed all of your floors with lemon, vinegar and sodium bicarbonate. She has chanted protection spells in several languages and saged everything in the place. She has also boosted the positive energy in your house with incense, tulsi plants, fresh flowers and white candles."

"Well, whoop-de do!"

"Look. You said yourself you have been untroubled by activity for a week. How was it working out for you before Diana came?"

She was right. What Jane had listed sounded ridiculous and useless to me but it was, in fact, working.

I made two cups of hot chocolate and went back over the discoveries of the day, starting with the snuff video. Jane whistled through her teeth.

"That is some freaky shit! And that is saying something coming from me!"

"It certainly is! Good news is though, it is proof that I was not inhabited by a spook and did not kill Gillian. Bad news is, if I had killed Gillian I would not have been stuck with the Haunted House, which as it is, I am. Jim says it will be the end of January at the soonest before he can even begin to offload it."

I then filled Jane in on the sad fate of young Alice.

"That is terrible. The poor girl." She paused.

"I tell you what! Let's go down to the cemetery tomorrow and have a word with her! Now you have your improved eyesight and everything!"

Jane looked disappointed when I told her that Alice was not buried there and that I had only seen the graves of Isabella Watson and Mary Ross.

"What about the others?"

"Well, Lydia Knox was swept out to sea, remains never found. Georgina MacCreith's family had money, so she is probably buried inside the Kirk. Victoria Paxman came from a very wealthy family. They probably have their own mausoleum out on their estate."

"Well then, I might as well start with Georgina MacCreith. At least she is nearby and indoors. I'll go first thing tomorrow."

I would say bright and early the next morning but a haar had come in off the sea, so it was more like dark and murky the next morning, I had a visit from Kathryn Bleakley, Chair of Governors.

"I am wearing my official hat, I'm afraid," she said taking off her enormous chunky knit scarf and kicking off her wellies in my hall.

"Well, have a cuppa anyway."

We sat down at the kitchen table crunching toast and sipping tea and finally she said, "I hope you will still make me tea and toast after I have delivered the Governors' message."

She looked genuinely worried.

"I'm afraid they want you to take a leave of absence for at least a term until all of this Gillian business is over."

I pointed out that I had been exonerated from having had any hand in Gillian's death with video proof of my innocence.

"Yes, they know all that but there is the inquest which will be months away, and then there is all that about the archives flooding..."

I poured more tea.

"Will I be on full pay?"

She looked relieved that I was taking it so well.

"Oh, yes of course! I realise it is all ridiculous and I am sure you know I fought it every inch of the way, but you know the governors."

I knew the governors all right.

"Kath, would you do me a favour and ask them if they would be prepared to make up my full pension if I agreed to go quietly? I only intended to do another five years anyway, so if they would ensure I did not lose out I could slip away and no more embarrassment."

She looked genuinely shocked and positively squeaked.

"No! No! You mustn't! What about the children? We will never get a replacement of your calibre."

"Well, I'm sorry, Kath, but that is your hard bun. Events of recent days have made me see the place in a new light. I don't think the children's parents will ever see me in the same light come to that. I think the shadow of Gillian's death will hang over me here forever, even after I'm gone most likely. There will always be those who say there is no smoke without fire and that I had a hand in it somewhere so that I could get her house in the will, though if they saw inside said house, they would soon change their minds."

"Why don't you think about it. Speak to Tom before you do anything rash. It will all blow over and we will be back to normal by Easter. You'll see!"

I said something platitudinous but before she left, she had agreed to put my offer to the Governors. There was one thing I knew that she did not. Tom has always had the utmost respect for my brain and my feelings. If I said I needed to do a thing he was always 100% behind me. Until Kath appeared out of the mist, I had not realised how strongly I felt that shaking the dust from my sandals was the right and only thing to do.

Not long after that, Jane wandered back in.

"Well, that was a right royal waste of time and effort!" she said, shrugging out of her afghan and letting it drop onto the floor.

"Georgina uncooperative?"

She put the kettle on then took a seat by the aga.

"I wouldn't know. I was interrupted by the Minister. He caught me at it and gave me the beginnings of a right royal Press button telling off."

"Just the beginnings?"

"Yes, I pulled a Diana on him. I let him see the silver gleam in my blue eyes and thereby persuaded him that he needed to Spring clean the kirk and that he had never met me in his life. He was last seen polishing the pews like a man possessed."

"Jane! For heaven's sake!"

"Exactly. He is doing it for Heaven's sake."

She made a cup of tea and snuggled into the armchair by the aga again.

"Point is we are no further forward. What did her inquest have to say?"

I had forgotten all about her report in the paper and decided to go down there at once for another interview with the charming Mrs Renfrew.

As soon as I opened the glazed Victorian door by its brass handle, I could hear her sighing.

"Back again, Dr Webster? To what do we owe the honour this time? More research, is it?"

"Yes, thank you, Mrs Renfrew," I replied with my most glittering smile, all the while thinking that if I were to be inclined to shove anyone under the express train to Inverness, she would have a very high spot on my list.

"1833 again, is it?"

"You have a good memory Mrs Renfrew, February please."

"Oh, I have an excellent memory Dr Webster," she said ominously, though the meaning was completely lost on me.

Soon I was again sitting in the first-floor office overlooking the Marketplace with a single volume of the Berwick Courant for 1833 resting on a green leather covered desk. The delightful Renfrew had given up her role as prison warder and seemed more than happy to leave me on my owney-oh. It took no time at all to find the record of the Inquest into the death of Georgina MacCreith.

- *The Court heard from Mr Alexander MacCreith, father of Miss Georgina MacCreith, that his daughter had been suffering from a cold which she had caught at the graveside of her friend Miss Alice Cameron. The family were of the opinion that Miss MacCreith was feeling a lot better, she was well enough to dress and repose on a chaise longue in the drawing room. Consequently, they allowed a visit from her music teacher, Count Beretsky and several of her friends who brought posies and chocolates. Count Beretsky played several light airs on his fiddle to entertain the invalid. The visitors left after about half an hour. At this time, Miss Georgina MacCreith was in high spirits and said she felt completely well. However, less than an hour later, Miss Georgina MacCreith was violently sick. She complained of dizziness and a severe headache. She started to breathe rapidly then she fell to the floor dead.*

Dr Alexander Jackson was called to the tragic scene and reported that Miss Georgina MacCreith was already deceased at the time of his arrival. He commented on the folly of exposing Miss MacCreith to the excitement of visitors when she was in a weakened physical condition. He attributed her demise to brain fever brought on by over-excitement. The Coroner, Mr Antony Brown Q.C. recorded a verdict of death by natural causes.

Two things were blatantly obvious: Dr Alexander Jackson was a moron and Georgina MacCreith had been poisoned by cyanide.

Back at the Ranch, I outlined what I had discovered to Jane. She was livid.

"The utter git! Bad enough to misdiagnose cyanide poisoning which is as obvious as the nose on your face. But to lay the blame for the death at the feet of her parents, who had done absolutely nothing wrong. The utter, utter git! Where is he buried? I'd love a word or two with him and they would all contain four letters!"

The darkness was closing in as we sat in the drawing room. I pulled the heavy velvet curtains across then threw another log onto the fire.

"So, it was the chocolates that did it then?"

"It seems like it. Did it say who gave her the chocs?"

"No, but they were all there, Beretsky and the remaining girls. It said she died an hour later. Would cyanide take that long?"

"No, but if the poison was in a single chocolate, it might take a while before she chose that particular one."

"Anybody could have chosen it."

"Do you really think our killer was bothered by this point?"

We sipped our wine in silence for a few moments.

"Where could the poison have come from? You can't just walk into a chemist and ask for cyanide."

"You probably could then. You could buy arsenic until the Pharmacy and Poisons Act put a stop to it and that was only in 1933."

"Still a fifteen-year-old girlie walking into a chemist and asking for cyanide would have set tongues wagging surely?"

"Not if she said her daddy wanted it to kill rats or a sick dog or something. Anyway, you can make your own cyanide at home."

"How?"

"By soaking almonds in water to get pure benzaldehyde, also known as oil of bitter almonds. You can still buy it on the internet, the place was probably awash with it in 1833. Almond flavour was very popular back in the day."

"Yes, that would fit nicely into a chocolate, and nobody would balk at the taste."

I got up and re-filled our glasses and threw another log on the fire. Jane stretched and said, "Who does that leave among the girl's inquest wise?"

"Inquest wise? Only Victoria Paxman and Lydia Knox. Oh, I forgot. I asked Jim Scott to fix me up with a look-see at the family archives at Paxman House. I might go there tomorrow but you would have to come with. I'm not keen for another flying around the room experience like I had in Langbridge."

"It's a deal. What's for supper?"

Chapter 12

Next morning, I rang Jim Scott. He had cleared it for me to examine the records in Paxman House. I asked if he thought Jane could come too and he said, "Darling, they don't give a rat's armpit about the old rubbish you want to root through. Ian Sinclair said that if it were up to him, you could take the lot and burn it then he could use the rooms for the Bed and Breakfast part of the business. So, I don't think taking Jane will be an issue. The place is locked up until March, but he has left the key under the stone lion on the right hand side of the door."

"What about alarms?"

"They haven't got one."

"Right."

"Toodle pip!"

Jane and I jumped into the car and set off northwest then left on the A1, right at the roundabout and straight on. In ten minutes, we had reached the gates of Paxman House. The place was built in dressed pink sandstone in a horseshoe shape. The main house was in the Palladian style with four impressive columns supporting a doric pediment at the top of a grand flight of stone steps. Every window had its symmetrical twin on the other side of the main door. Jane set off up the steps.

"No, Jane. We don't want the main house we want the kitchen wing on the right there."

Sure enough, there were two modest little sandstone lions either side of the door and the promised key was where Jim said it would be. I turned the lock, and we entered the section of the building used for admin purposes only which did not form part of the tour for visitors. I gave a call, but answer came there none. As expected, we were alone. Our footsteps rang in the silence as we stepped along the terracotta tiled corridor and up the stone staircase. This part of the house had been the kitchens and servants' quarters. Every expense had been spared. The servants' quarters now housed the archives of the house if you could call the jumble of ledgers, diaries, bills and letters tumbling out of old orange boxes and beer crates an archive. Luckily, the jumble was at least stored more or less in date order.

Jane had brought a pair of rubber gloves from my kitchen. For someone who spent her life up to her elbows in other people's brains, she was surprisingly finicky about getting her hands dirty. We heaved centuries of boxes and crates out of the way until finally we arrived at the early eighteen hundreds. Then the real work began. Looking for letters, or if we were lucky a diary, from 1833 was literally like looking for the proverbial needle in a haystack. We found endless receipts, stock records, wages books, tenants' rent lists, accounts, bills, ledgers and then Jane screamed. The most blood curdling scream I have ever heard in my life.

She had come across a dead mouse in the box she was sorting through. I picked it up and threw it into the corner.

"Oh my God!" she shrieked. "You touched that with your bare hands!"

"Jane, it is only a mummified mouse. For somebody who has spent her life in other people's gorey bits I can't believe you are going all wobbly over a mouse. Dead mice, rats, birds, bats are all par for the course for an archivist. Welcome to my world!"

"That is disgusting. When can we leave? I'm getting hungry and it is colder than a witch's tit in here."

"You ought to know."

"Oh ha-de-ha!"

"We'll give it another quarter of an hour. We can always come back tomorrow."

"No bloody way!" She grabbed the next crate with gusto and started ferreting through it at speed.

Jane's allotted time drew to a close and we had found precisely nothing, I said as much.

"OK, Jane, let's call it a day."

"Yippee! Maybe we should try tackling this my way."

"How do you mean?"

"I mean I talk to dead people. Let's start with the two who drowned together, Isabella and Margaret. Two for the price of one. I'll look out my trowel."

"Oh my God, Jane! You are not thinking of digging them up!"

"No! You idiot, it helps me get in touch. You'll see this afternoon. We'll go about 3pm. Dawn or dusk is best and you know me and early mornings. Now let's go and eat for God's sake! I am starving!"

****

Shortly before 3pm, I was back in the desolate graveyard overlooking a grey and ominous North Sea with the light fading fast. A light mist was meandering amongst the stones. I had warned Jane about the long, damp grass so she had rushed out to spend a fortune on Hunter wellies and a Barbour jacket. The natural world and Jane did not mix. I could hear her grumbling along behind me as I followed my usual track through the grasses to the location of the gravestones of the two drowned girls.

When we got there, she pulled a silver trowel out of her designer backpack (also new) and approached the stones.

"This will be an experience for you, Kate. You should probably stand back a bit. They can sense nervous newbies."

I was more than happy to stand well back. I would rather not be there at all! As it was, I plumped for standing in the lea of one of those ancient, tall gravestones. This one so weathered and lichen covered that it was impossible to read the inscriptions on the other side.

Jane lifted the silver trowel which bore the engraving.

'Presented to the Right Honourable K.S. Avery M.P.
On the occasion of the laying of the foundation stone of the Unionist Club.
World's End, Sheffield, 1824'.

She knocked three times on both gravestones then she stood back. I was underwhelmed.

"Is that it?"

"What do you mean?"

"Well, no going into a trance or chanting spells in a long dead language?"

"Oh, shut up. Here they come."

Well, I couldn't see anything, and I have to say I was very glad about it, then there was a certain thickening of the mist by the graves and suddenly, there they were! Two girls in white eighteenth century nightdresses, their arms wrapped around each other. I felt sick. I thought I would have been terrified by their ghastly, ghostly aspect but they were just like ordinary girls, albeit they looked as if they had been filmed in black and white only. They were clearly afraid and gave off an air of sorrow that made me feel like all the joy had just been sucked out of the world.

"Hello, Margaret. Hello, Isabella. My name is Jane and this is my friend Kate."

I had no idea she was going to bandy my name around the undead and I was not best pleased about it!

"We really need your help. We are trying to find out if someone was responsible for your deaths and those of your friends. Can you tell us about that?"

The two ghost girls began nodding furiously, all the while looking towards the sea in sheer terror. Then they began speaking, finishing each other's sentences in the way of best friends in a rush to tell a tale.

"We had gone to the boat house to speak privately."

"We got into the boat to sit away from everyone because we knew who was responsible and—"

"We didn't know what to do or who would believe us, and it was so windy we—"

"We did not hear—"

"We were hit from behind with the oar from the boat and pushed out into the flood."

As they were speaking, the wind had suddenly arisen and the skeletal winter trees were thrashing their arms about and squealing as they rubbed against each other. The wind became stronger and stronger in a matter of moments. The girls cried out and disappeared. Still the wind increased until it was roaring, and I could barely see Jane amid a whirl of dead leaves and torn up white grass. The roaring and whirling continued to gather strength until it was near impossible to catch my breath even though I was safely crouched behind the gravestone. Jane weighs next to nothing and, being caught out in the open, the force of the gale was enough to lift her off her feet. However, any thought that this was some natural weather event was put beyond question when Jane was thrown from side to side against the current of the wind. It was as if she were a tiny doll in the fist of a bratty toddler, she was zoomed from right to left and back again.

Suddenly there was total calm, and Jane dropped from a height of about twelve feet to land in a heap on the wet grass. As she fell every dead leaf and dry grass stalk fell in unison with her.

I rushed out from behind the gravestone. Jane was lying totally still, half-covered in leaves and grasses. One of her new wellingtons was gone. Her limbs were at all angles. Her eyes were closed.

****

Chapter 13

Next morning, *The Berwick Gazette* bore the headline, 'Twister hits Berwick' and it told the tale of the unusual weather event. Our names were not included it just said, "Two elderly women were visiting the graveyard at the time of the event and were caught in the whirlwind."

Jane, sipping coffee from a mug in one hand whilst holding a bag of frozen peas on her black eye with the other almost choked.

"Elderly! Elderly! Bloody cheek! We are in the prime of our lives and a decade away from our pension thanks to sodding governments of all sodding stripes! Elderly! I'll sue!"

"Well, it doesn't give our names and in all fairness, we were not looking our best when that reporter spotted us in the distance running from the scene. The paper goes on to say that the twister was caused by warm humid air clashing with cold dry air causing an updraft. What do you think caused it?"

"Well, it wasn't an updraft. I can tell you that!" she said putting down her mug and rubbing her ribs. "It was obviously him again, wasn't it? This is the same trick he pulled on that Headmaster at Langbridge Towers."

I had been thinking about that.

"You know, Jane, I have been thinking about that and I am sure there was more than one presence there."

"Oh great! Just what we need, another one!" she picked up her coffee mug again.

"No. I mean there was one that tried to help. I was so shocked and worried about Bill that it has taken me a few days to get the whole thing straight in my mind, but when I think back there was another force that was trying to help me get my bag back. It even partook in a battle with the other one throwing trunks at it."

"Maybe it was a resident ghost at the school that did not want another ghost muscling in on its turf. Any chance of me popping in for a chat."

"I doubt it. Bill was having the attic exorcised and nailed up."

"Probably just as well."

Jane got a call in the small hours and drove off in my car to Newcastle…young man not wearing a seatbelt had gone through the window of his car when it skidded on the ice, A1 just south of Morpeth. Diana had also vanished…some trouble with a wailing wraith in a shooting box out on a far Northumberland moor.

I wandered down to the offices of the *Berwick Gazette* again, got my usual welcome from Mrs Renfrew and settled down with the newspaper for 6 April 1833. Victoria Paxman was the last of the girls to bite the dust and she did so literally on 13 March 1833, ten days before the Count was bushwhacked and killed.

The Court heard from Sir Alistair Paxman, father of Miss Victoria Rose Paxman, that his daughter had been taking tea with her mother, her piano teacher, Count Beretsky and a school-friend in the drawing room at Paxman House which is located on the first floor. When the time came for the visitors to depart Victoria left her Mama in the drawing room and started to walk down the marble staircase to the entrance hall. Victoria was leading the way linking the arm of her friend as the two were engrossed in conversation. Count Stanislav Beretsky was walking a few steps behind. It is assumed that Miss Paxman caught her foot in the hem of her dress. Her friend was not strong enough to save her from the impetus of the fall which resulted in her tumbling to her death.

Dr Alexander Jackson was called to the tragic scene and reported that Miss Victoria Rose Paxman was already deceased at the time of his arrival. He pronounced the cause of death to be a massive blow to the cranium owing to the striking of the head at speed upon the marble floor of the vestibule. Miss Paxman had also suffered several broken bones as the result of striking the edges of the stairs in the course of the fall. The Coroner, Mr Antony Brown Q.C. recorded a verdict of accidental death.

Poor Victoria. The Count must have pushed them both from behind but the 'friend' must have been near the banister and able to cling on. The friend had to have been Lydia, there was no one else left alive in the group. Why didn't she say something? Maybe she thought if she kept schtum, he wouldn't kill her.

I packed up and, with as much insincerity as I could muster, wished Mrs Renfrew the compliments of the season then headed home.

There was still no sign of my car in the drive. Either it was a long job or, more likely, Jane had met some old medical pals and gone for a seasonal drink and would stay over in Newcastle for the night. The phone rang. It was Jim Scott. A client had given him a voucher for dinner for two at the Marton Meadow Hotel and did I want to join him. Suddenly starving, I jumped at the chance and went to get dressed up for a change. This Festive Season had been seriously lacking in fest, time to forget it all and raid my wardrobe for a touch of sparkle!

When I returned, there was a car in my drive, but it was not mine. Diana's purple people carrier was neatly parked by the gate. The Christmas tree lights were burning brightly, and smoke was curling from the chimney.

"How did you get in?" I asked.

"All part of the job, darling."

"Witchery requires breaking and entering 101, does it?"

"Not that job, darling. Police personnel have to be able to enter premises where an on-going crime is suspected or in the case of a death. We all have a little lock-pick kit."

"Really."

"Yes. Jane has filled me in on your disappointing trip to Paxman House. Would you like me to come with you tomorrow so that you can search again?"

I had been itching to get back to search again and who better to do that with than the biggest spook scarer this side of eternity? We would go in the morning.

Luckily, Diana was an early riser, probably all those years of 6–2 shift work. We were on the road by 8am and walking across the circular lawn in front of the Servants' Block at Paxman House by 8:15. It was a clear and frosty morning and the grass crunched satisfactorily beneath the feet. I retrieved the key from under the lion and in we went. Diana paused just inside the door and took a few deep breaths.

"Nothing here to worry about," she announced so we trekked along the terracotta tiled corridor and up the stone staircase. Once inside the pokey bedroom, I got stuck into the crates we had dragged to the front of the pile the other day. Diana did not. When I turned around, she was pulling a stick from her capacious handbag.

"You look your way and I'll look mine, darling," she said beginning to wave a forked twig around.

If you want anything done, you might as well do it yourself; I was thinking when I heard her feet pattering off into the distance. Maybe she needed the loo which was awkward because the loo was in the opposite wing, I did not have a key for that. I peeped out of the door only to see her on bended knee next to the door at the end of the corridor.

"That's the door into the main house, Diana. It will be locked and anyway the loo isn't there, it is in the other wing."

There was a little click. She turned smiling.

"I do not need the loo darling. I am on the trail of your girl's diary. It is in here somewhere." As she spoke, she had turned the handle and waddled into the main house bedroom corridor.

Ian Sinclair would have a dippy fit! Mooching through old paperwork was one thing but breaking and entering into the main house was quite another.

"Come back, Diana! We are not allowed in there!"

I doubt if she even heard me. By now, she was at the far end of the corridor. She held a forked twig before her as she marched along and as she approached a large wardrobe against the wall the twig suddenly dipped.

"This is it!" she yelled.

There was no option other than to go in after her. This would look great in the papers, not only accused of shoving my secretary under a train, vandalism, and arson but now breaking into an historic building. We had better not get caught.

By the time I reached her, Diana had used her not inconsiderable hips to barge the wardrobe to one side. This house was known for its collection of priceless Chippendale furniture, this was most likely a Chippendale armoire she was manhandling.

"Diana! For God's sake that's Chippendale. Leave it alone!"

But she kept on barging and the armoire kept on moving until at last we could see what had been hidden behind it. It was another bedroom door. A hidden bedroom door.

"The hazel never lets me down," she said sweeping the cobwebs away from the door surround with her sleeve.

I know I should have insisted upon leaving right that second but who can resist the idea of a secret room and its possible contents. If Diana was right and Victoria Paxman's diary was in there, it was worth the risk. That diary could hold the key and end all of this.

The door was locked but Diana made short work of that.

"Ready?" she said.

Chapter 14

Jane was back when we reached my house in Berwick. I couldn't wait to tell her what Diana had done and what we had found and what had happened then. Diana seemed bored and wandered off for a bath. Jane and I sat in front of the Aga with a coffee, and I told her all.

When Diana pushed the door great hinges of cobwebs yawed into the room with us. The vision before us was breathtaking. What we saw was an untouched *chambre de demoiselle*, a young lady's bedroom, which had clearly not been touched since 1833 when Victoria died. Her parents must have had the room locked on the day of her death and ordered the armoire pushed in front of the door. Nobody had dared move the armoire in all that time and probably the existence of the room had passed from living memory a century ago.

Clearly, Victoria had been a much-loved child. The room was splendid. It reminded me of Ursule Mirouët's phrase 'In this room you might breathe in the perfume of heaven'. It was very pink and would have suited my daughter down to the ground when she went through her Barbie phase. The walls were painted white with floor to ceiling panels of rose, water silk outlined with ornate gilded carvings of roses and swags in the French style. There was a white marble Italianate fireplace with a fire screen also depicting roses that the poor girl had probably executed herself. A fabulous, Venetian chandelier was suspended from a plasterwork ceiling depicting yet more roses. It looked like the ghost of a chandelier, shrouded as it was in grey cobwebs.

A cream turkey carpet with a border of pink roses and other flowers in vibrant colours covered most of the floor. It had a deep velvety pile and, as we crossed it, it held the shape of our footprints in the dust of centuries. Victoria's bed was set into an arched alcove at the back of the room. There were tasselled pink toile curtains and matching bed covers. Another narrow bed of wrought iron, which must have been for a governess or nurse to sleep in was located in the far corner. It had a plain pink silk counterpane and canopy.

There was a chaise longue and an armchair upholstered in deep rose velvet. A dressing table in a serpentine shape with cream damask curtains around the bottom. A small tea table, probably Chippendale, in the rococo style with four matching spindly chairs. The door of a large wardrobe stood slightly ajar and numerous silken dresses could be glimpsed. They were mostly blue and white, the colours of marriage, as was customary for young ladies at the time.

We approached the bed in silent reverence. There lay a pristine early Victorian doll. Most early nineteenth century dolls, even those belonging to Queen Victoria, had heads like the tops of clothes-pegs; perfect spheres with painted on hair and features. Not this doll; she had been sculpted from some light wood. She had a nose and even eye lids and a perfect, tapered face. Her hands were similarly detailed. She was dressed in a lilac silk gown of the latest fashion. On her feet were tiny black leather boots and delicate blonde ringlets fell from a straw bonnet decorated with teeny violets. Whose hair and eyesight were sacrificed for the making of this rich girl's plaything?

Diana remained by the bed doing her communing thing while I checked the dressing table. I thought at first that it had been draped in net but at close inspection it was spidery handiwork. I pulled back the webs to reveal a Sevres vase of long dead roses and the contents of her dressing table. There was a set of hairbrushes and a mirror with blackened silver backs. In the centre was a little jewel box of dark red tortoiseshell in a sarcophagus shape with brass ball feet and matching lock escutcheon. To one side lay a small pile of leather-bound improving books and there beside them, at last, Victoria Paxman's diary.

"What the hell do you think you are playing at?"

Back at home, I told Jane what had happened at Paxman House and how Ian Sinclair had caught us in Victoria's bedroom. Jane wandered off to ring Jim Scott to see what he could do.

"He says to leave it with him. He and Ian go back a long way so it should be fine." She flopped down onto the sofa and propped her slipper socks on the arm. "Who do we have left? Are there any other girls we have not looked into yet? We could investigate them while we await the fruits of Jim's labours."

I checked my list.

"Only one left, Lydia Knox. She was the last one to die. She fell into the river first of April 1833. The Count could not have been responsible for her death though, he had been dead a fortnight when she went."

"Even so it is a bit of a co-incidence that a fortnight after his death she tops herself."

"Oh, my giddy aunt! Jane, I have been the biggest idiot on the planet! I know what this is about! I think she had a crush on the Count! Adolescent teenagers have violent feelings they cannot control. I think she was besotted with him and when her daddy had him killed, she could not go on."

"Was she the one whose mother threw herself off the roof?"

"Yes, and the coroner's report said that Mrs Knox was pregnant. Also, according to the priest's housekeeper at the time the father was probably not Mr Knox. Poor girl, she had been present when at least some of her friends died and then her own mother. Her crush on the Count was probably the only thing keeping her going."

"So, she was left motherless, with no friends and maybe she discovered that her lover-boy had been sleeping with her mother and what her father had done to the Count. Ouch! Poor girl. Do you think we should have a word with her? Where is she buried?"

"She isn't. Her body was never found. Swept out to sea."

"Right, well then, I'll have to call her back from Davey Jones' locker. Where is Diana? This could be a big job."

"Diana got a frantic call from some poor soul who has just bought a haunted hotel that has a green slime problem, so she took off."

"I am just wondering if Lydia's ghost might be just the ticket for clearing your house. I would think her crush will have well and truly worn off by now. She might be just the kiddy to drag him out of your mansion and boot him towards the throne of judgement. Put the kettle on, I'll send out for pizza."

Sitting on a bollard on Berwick quayside at 1.30 in the morning deep in frosty December was not my idea of a festive night out. I was wearing a hat, scarf, coat and gloves with another hat, scarf, coat and gloves on top. This was partly to disguise myself in case anyone came along and partly to stop my vital organs from freezing into a cannibal ready meal. Despite being the width of a pencil, Jane never felt the cold and only wore winter coats if they were in fashion.

I had seen her do her thing a few times when we were young. I caught the stage act once and she freely admitted she had jazzed it up so that the punters felt they had had their money's worth. She was doing her real thing now. It reminded me of *When Harry Met Sally* with the sound turned off. There was certainly a lot of blowing out and sucking in of breath. I sat silent, like I said, I had witnessed this before. It seemed to cause a vibration in the air you couldn't identify and a heaviness as if someone had just dialled up the earth's gravity knob. I was suddenly very conscious of the fact that I was sitting with my back to the loathsome house. I had the feeling that eyes were boring into my spine.

Jane stopped, approached the edge of the quay and beckoned me over. At first, the gentle slap of the river against the quay wall was all that I saw and then it began.

The water started to suck away from itself in a circle. Weirdly, concentric rings of water started moving inwards as if showing a video of throwing a rock into water were being shown backwards. It had an oily, unreal appearance. The water became completely still again and then there was a sucking noise and a hole appeared in the water, sucking and swirling downwards like a mini whirlpool. Then the hair appeared.

It was long, wavy, light brown, mousy, writhing over the river surface like snakes. It made me feel nauseous but fascinated at the same time. All the while, the water had been sucking downwards, now it suddenly reversed as if trying to spit something out. That something was a head.

Luckily, the head was looking the other way, across the river, it was bad enough to see it from the side – not that it was rotted or anything, it looked fresh, the skin young, peaches and cream, it was a girl of about 15. There was no sound from her gaping mouth, but she was clearly screaming.

The river spat her out. She rose like a ghoulish Lady of the Lake. Her arms were flapping as if to stop herself falling into the river. We were watching the whole thing in slow motion and in reverse. Her hair dried and seaweed fell away from her garments as she ascended backwards through the air. Next thing we knew she was standing on the quay beside us but thankfully, she seemed oblivious of our presence. She was wearing an ivory morning dress of the period, suitable to her age and station. It was delicate, silken, it had the typical wide gigot sleeves, large collar and high waist fashionable at the time. She had white stockings and tiny, pink, satin shoes on her feet.

Her body suddenly jerked forward then she approached the house, backwards of course. She seemed to be struggling violently but there was nobody there, nobody I could see at any rate.

Up the steps to the house she went, writhing and wriggling all the way. Her hands pulled at her hair as if trying to dislodge the grip of an assailant. The door flung itself open. She staggered backwards over the thresh. The door wrenched shut.

In a second, the ringing in my ears stopped, gravity returned to normal, the waves kissed the quay. Jane broke the silence.

"Oh shit!"

"Oh shit? What do you mean oh shit! I thought that was supposed to be it! I thought the idea was that Lydia came back from the other side went in there and kicked his arse to judgement. That is what you said Jane, correct me if I'm wrong here!"

Jane was still staring at the bleak, silent, grim house.

"That should not have happened. We have miscalculated here somewhere."

"No shit, Sherlock!"

Jane turned towards me.

"This isn't an exact science you know. It isn't all clear cut and crystal, or any idiot could do it. You for instance!"

I spun away from the house.

"I'm the idiot? How am I the idiot here? You are supposed to be the expert in this area, Jane. You are the Madame Arcati in this scenario and as far as I can see just about as useless!"

Jane hated being called Madame Arcati and I knew it.

"You, Kate dear, are an idiot because you are the Pliny in this scenario. You are supposed to be the greatest historian since BC bugger all! You are the one who was supposed to have researched the relationship between him and Lydia not me."

I hated my academic ability being questioned and she knew it.

"I did research it! You know I did! It took me days going through newspapers, letters, diaries of just about every boring old bugger in Berwick and let me tell you that Berwick in 1833 was just about the universal capital of boring old buggers! I found out everything there was to know!"

Jane snapped back.

"Well, it's a shame you didn't find out that, Lydia, despite her mother getting knocked up by him and her subsequent suicide and the deaths of her friends, despite throwing herself in the river…was truly, madly, deeply, head-over-heels, from here to eternity in love with the bastard!"

I hadn't thought of that.

"Oh shit!"

Jane gave a sigh of exasperation.

"That's what I said."

I sat down on a bollard.

"So what does that mean now?"

Jane sat on the next bollard.

"It means we have twice the problem we had before."

I stared back at the dark and still-silent house.

"Well, we learned one thing anyway, Jane. That was the weirdest suicide ever. It is obvious that she did not go gently into that goodnight."

Jane shook her head.

"You realise what this means? We have got the whole thing wrong. The Count cannot have killed her because she did not die until weeks after her uncle cut him up and turned him into souvenirs."

"And if he did not kill her, then the serial child killer was still on the loose and maybe the Count was innocent all along."

Jane pulled out her mobile phone.

"I'm going to make a call."

"Who ya gonna call ghostbusters?"

Jane paused mid-tap.

"In a way. I'm sending for the real Madame Arcati and the Girls in the Band."

****

Next morning, I was experiencing the prickly feeling I sometimes get as if something is jangling just beyond the range of my hearing. I prepared myself for piano playing or the flying of tins of beans, but nothing happened. The house had been quiet and peaceful ever since Diana did her thing, and yet.

There was something wrong. I had got something wrong. For a start, Lydia clearly did not kill herself. Even backwards and in slow motion, it was obvious that someone threw her into the river long after the Count was mincemeat. Were there two killers? Was the Count innocent of all charges? I decided to go back to the beginning and lay out all the key pieces of evidence and look at them with a dispassionate historian's eye. I began to realise that the dramatic circumstances in which this evidence had been gathered had possibly, or let's face it, probably skewed my reasoning. It was difficult to remain objective when some serial killer from beyond the grave is trying to bump you off. Even if he is doing it to a soundtrack of Chopin.

We had a bite to eat and then I told Jane about my plan to review the story so far. She said two heads were better than one and she would try to see if there was a link I had missed.

Back to the beginning I went. When was the beginning? The Halloween party? That introduced me to the count and the sad tale of his demise but in that case, he was more sinned against than sinning. I decided to begin with the confession I had read out at the party. It was only two months ago but it seemed like years.

My daughter came to me two days before the death of her Polish piano tutor, Count Stanislav Beretsky. She told me that he was after her affections and had taken liberties that I cannot bear to set down here. Times are hard and I had no difficulty in finding four men to waylay the pianist and beat him. I gave a special instruction to break his hands. This was done but the Count staggered back to Berwick, to my house on the Old Quay Walls. I denied him admittance. It was winter. He died on the doorstep.

I was wrong. God forgive me. What I have done was for all our good even hers. God have mercy on us.

"I wonder what he meant by that last bit?" mused Jane.

"I'm beggared if I know. Maybe that he realised it was wrong to kill the Count but that it was in the interests of everyone in Berwick to stop him killing anyone else."

"Possibly. We should come back to it though after we have seen the other evidence. What's next?"

"Well, the next piece of evidence is Gillian's suicide note. I have a copy here somewhere. Yes, here it is."

He has chosen you. I realised it that night you came to the party at my house, when he played the piano for you and

laid his hand upon your shoulder. He is yours now and I have nothing further to live for.

I have left my will with MacCreith and Scott in Bridge Street. The house is yours; you have to accept it. I have left the dog locked in the house to make sure you have to go inside as soon as possible.

He is waiting for you. He is cursed already but with my last breath I curse you.

Gillian Mary Morris

Jane grinned. "You make a really great impression on people, don't you?"

"She was certifiably insane remember!"

"Yes, OK. She seems to have believed that the Count had given up on her, cast her aside etc., and that you were the other woman. She was obviously besotted with the Count's ghost. This is some creepy shit, even in my neck of the woods."

"And that is saying something! Anyway, she seems to be saying that the ghost of the Count was haunting the house and she was well aware of him, may even have seen him. Possibly, she was seeing him all the time and he was clearly playing the piano for her."

"But he saw something in you that made him swap allegiances."

"The creepiest part is that she did her husband in for this dead guy."

I ferreted through the paperwork again and found the copy of Gillian's confession to her husband's murder.

"She reckons she waited until he was up a ladder by the upstairs landing, and she pushed him over the balustrade.

I Gillian Mary Morris do hereby confess to the murder of my husband George Arthur Morris. He was on top of a ladder by the upstairs landing checking the cracks in the ceiling when I suddenly became overwhelmed. I was not myself anymore. I pushed the ladder towards the balustrade and George fell down to the hall floor. His neck was broken. I came to myself and could not believe what I had done but there he was, dead on the hall floor, red blood on the black and white tiles. I loved him. Why did I do it?

Gillian Mary Morris

"Well, that answers one question anyway," said Jane.

"It does?"

"Of course! She was clearly possessed! Some spirit had spitefully nipped into her body to kill the husband!"

"Oh no! Don't tell me the Count's ghost was jealously in love with Gillian!"

"I seriously doubt it," said Jane looking puzzled, "Usually, well, always really, spirits stick to their own sex. It is vastly more likely that Gillian was possessed by a female entity."

"Whose? The only females in the house were Lydia and her mother."

Jane continued with the puzzled look, reached for a notepad and made some notes then said, "Crack on then, what is the next piece of evidence?"

I ferreted through the pile again.

"Well, after that all we have is the coroner's reports from the newspapers and the notes the parish priest made."

We decided to do all of the coroner's reports in order of death. We started with Alice Cameron. I read out the relevant section to Jane.

Mr Robert Cameron gave evidence that his daughter, a child of 15, had been enjoying her birthday party with her friends. They had a party tea and as a special treat Miss Cameron's piano teacher, Count Stanislav Beretsky had attended the soiree to play a little waltz written especially for the occasion. As the party was drawing to its close, the girls went upstairs to retrieve their cloaks from Miss Cameron's bedroom. It was at this time that Miss Cameron must have lost her footing and sadly, her dress billowed out towards the fire. Miss Cameron's party dress was made of a pink tissue which was instantly ablaze. Some of the young ladies ran for help whilst others utilised pillows to beat out the flames.

The Coroner, Mr Antony Brown Q.C. commended the actions of the young ladies: Misses Georgina MacCreith Margaret Ross, Victoria Paxman, Lydia Knox and Isabella Watson before reaching a verdict of accidental death.

"The striking thing here, Jane, is that the Count could not have been in the room when Alice's dress caught fire, because a man would not have been permitted into the bedroom of a young lady in those days. Certainly not without the presence of her parents."

"Maybe this was just an accident."

"Maybe, but it seems just too coincidental. It was the start of the deaths of a small group of friends: Alice, Georgina, Isabella, Margaret, Victoria, Lydia – all of whom died in suspicious circumstances."

Jane made more notes on her pad. "Who was next?"

"Georgina MacCreith." Fourteen days later, she had a cold.

Miss MacCreith was feeling a lot better, she was well enough to dress and repose on a chaise longue in the drawing room. Consequently, they allowed a visit from her music teacher, Count Beretsky and several of her friends who brought posies and chocolates. Count Beretsky played some light airs on his fiddle to entertain the invalid. The visitors left after about half an hour. At this time Miss MacCreith was in high spirits and said she felt completely well. However, less than an hour later Miss MacCreith was violently sick. She complained of dizziness and a severe headache. She started to breathe rapidly then she fell to the floor dead.

"She was the one who was poisoned with that almond-flavoured cyanide stuff. Read what it says about the chocolate again."

"*Several of her friends who brought posies and chocolates.*"

"**Several of her friends** not the Count," said Jane dramatically.

"He may have been included in the general 'friends' category, but I take your point."

"Who's next?"

I rummaged again and found Isabella and Margaret.

These were the girls you spoke to. They drowned a week after Georgina died.

'*Both young ladies bore wounds about the head and face*'.

That chimes with what the girls told you about being hit with an oar.

The last person to see the two young ladies alive was their friend, Miss Lydia Knox, who saw the young ladies walking arm in arm towards the boathouse in the grounds of Langbridge Academy on the afternoon of their disappearance. Miss Knox followed the girls but before she could catch up to them, she saw them both step into a rowboat and cast off from the shore. Miss Knox ran to admonish them but by the time she reached the riverbank the boat had been swept out to the midst of the stream. Miss Knox saw the girls stand up shouting for help and at that the boat swayed and the two young ladies were knocked into the river. Miss Knox ran back to the school to seek help but by the time she found assistance the two girls had been swept away.

Jane turned over her pad to show me that all she had written was the name Lydia over and over again.

"She did it, Kate! The Count is innocent! It was Lydia all along!"

Why did I not see that? Possibly because he had been irritating the hell out of me with the endless Chopin etc., etc.

"Oh, Jane! I think you may be right. If it is her, then a lot of unexplained things suddenly fall into place but, a fifteen-year-old female serial killer? Just to be sure let's continue to examine the evidence we have left. Here is Victoria Paxman's report."

It is assumed that Miss Paxman caught her foot in the hem of her dress. Her friend was not strong enough to save her from the impetus of the fall which resulted in her tumbling to her death.

Jane was literally bouncing on her chair.

"Her friend was Lydia! It had to be Lydia there was no bugger else left!"

It all fit but, a fifteen-year-old female serial killer?

"What about motive, Jane? Why would she suddenly turn on her friends and systematically wipe them out?"

"It's obvious, Kate! She was head over heels in love with the Count and did not want any competition. Your very words to me were, 'these fifteen-year-old girls had lived very sheltered lives. The Count must have seemed like James Bond and Lancelot rolled into one for them' and 'Adolescent teenagers have violent feelings they cannot control'. All of her classmates were taking lessons from him to be accomplished young ladies. When he singled out Alice by writing a waltz for her birthday, he was signing her death warrant. The same applied when he played especially for Georgina when she was ill. Then, having bumped off two competitors for his attention, it was easy peasy to clear the field killing two birds with one stone with Margaret and Isabella. She was the only one there. She followed them all right. They must have suspected her and had gone to discuss their suspicions and what to do about them in private at the boathouse. Lydia sneaked up behind them, silently lifted an oar and battered them to death before shoving the boat out into the river and then crying wolf!"

"I still think we should keep going through the evidence objectively. We will see if anything else supports your theory."

"OK. What's next?"

"The notes made by the priest." Here they are:

"No sooner had Mrs O'Neill left the room than Mrs Knox grabbed my arm and, looking earnestly into my face said, How could this be? It is my fault. I am her mother after all. It is my fault! Oh, wickedness, wickedness! I allowed him liberties I should never…God forgive me. What am I to do? Now it is all too late. I have to tell the truth but what about Lydia? What will become of her if the truth is known? Yet I cannot go on with this awful lie, this terrible secret."

"So basically, she seems to be admitting she had a bit of a dalliance at the very least with the Count and she was worried if it got out there would be damage to Lydia's reputation."

Jane shook her head.

"I don't read it that way at all. I think she is admitting to the affair, fair enough, but when she says, '*Now it is all too late. I have to tell the truth but what about Lydia? What will become of her if the truth is known? Yet I cannot go on with this awful lie, this terrible secret*'. She could be saying she has found out that Lydia is the killer, and she is going to dob her into the police but she is worried she will hang. Where is the report on her death?"

It was easy to find as I had almost come to the bottom of the pile.

"She died about a fortnight after Victoria." Here it is:

"Mrs Knox was still living at the time of his arrival despite major injuries resulting from her fall from the roof.

Mrs Knox said the name of her daughter, Lydia, repeatedly and then passed away in the Doctor's arms. Mr James Knox gave evidence on behalf of his daughter, a child of 15, that Mother and Daughter had been taking the air on the widow's walk above the house when a sudden gust of wind caught Mrs Knox' skirts and hurled her to the ground."

"See? Mrs Knox said the name of her daughter, Lydia repeatedly; she was trying to tell them that the little bitch had thrown her own mother off the roof. You can just imagine how livid Lydia was when she found out that while she was killing five of her friends so that she could have him, her mother was banging the Count under her very nose!"

"So, she suggests a nice walk on the roof terrace to have a heart to heart with Mummy and then she grabs her and pushes her over." I suddenly had a thought and checked the dates. "The Count was murdered three days later. Looks like she wanted her revenge on him too for passing her over in favour of Mummy, so she told her daddy that the Count..." I reached for the Knox confession.

'...*was after her affections and had taken liberties that I cannot bear to set down here.*'

"So, she wound Daddy up to have the Count killed."

"Real piece of work, isn't she?"

I still couldn't get my head around it. It was all interpretation and I said so to Jane. Could this all be the work of a spoilt brat having a mega-tantrum?

Jane poured us both a brandy. "What else have you got on the pile?"

I rooted through the remaining papers. "Just my notes about what happened in the archives and at Longridge."

"Read me the bit about the battle with the trunks at Longridge."

Right-ho:

What happened next was bizarre even by my current standards. As far as I could see through the whirling paper, a battle broke out for possession of the trunk. As it was invisibly lifted and carried towards one door, other trunks were lifted and hurled at it until it fell, only for it to be instantly lifted and pulled the other way. Trunks flew unaided back and forth banging chunks out of the plaster and the floorboards. I had to roll this way and that as I tried to make my way to the hatch dragging my bag behind me. I was nearly there when whatever it was must have realised that I had the goods in my bag then a three-way tussle broke out between the two entities, for want of a better word, and me. One of them did seem to be on my side in this but the two of us together were no match for the other one.

"There are two of them of course! Of course!"

"Jane, I told you that and you said it was probably a resident ghost having a turf war with the one I brought with me."

Jane took a sip of her brandy.

"It was him!"

"Who?"

"Don't you see it was the Count!"

"Well, I think we knew that all along."

"No, you twit! It was the Count who was helping you! The ghastly Lydia was trying to stop you gaining access to the records that might give her away, just like she did in the Archives!"

"The little cow! She nearly killed me with those flying trunks."

Jane laughed.

"It's worse than that! She nearly killed me in the graveyard! Shake me about like a puppet, would she? That bitch is going down!"

There was a token ring of the doorbell and Jim Scott fell in. I wondered if the Count was back to his old tricks, but one whiff of his breath and the cause proved to be spirits of a more worldly kind.

"This is all your fault, Kate. Next time you get caught breaking and entering leave me out of it."

I helped him off with his coat and sat him next to the Aga while I went to make coffee.

"I don't see how you getting as nissed as a pewt is my fault."

He gazed at me through yellow eyes.

"It is your fault because I had to take Ian Sinclair out to dinner to schmooze him into not pressing charges. Of course, he chose Tattersall Castle."

I paused with the coffee pot in mid-air.

"Tattersall Castle! That place costs a fortune! It's £25 for a bowl of soup."

Jim put his sore head in his hands.

"You have no idea. He chomped his way through the card from soup to nuts. We had amuse-bouche in the library with sherry then we moved into the dining room: Cullen skink with a malt whiskey on the side, turbot with fresh grated truffles, caviar and a bottle of Domaine Leflaive Batard Montrachet;

T-bone steak with roast seasonal veg and a bottle of Chateau Margaux; Cranachan with a cheeky little desert wine; a cheeseboard with a Sandeman 33 port. Of course, we adjourned to the library again for coffee, hand-made chocolates, napoleon brandy and cigars."

Jane had been busy drawing flow diagrams on her notepad but even she blenched at the thought of the cost.

"Bloody hell fire Jim that must have cost a mint!"

He turned his bleary gaze towards her.

"That was not the end of it. Obviously, neither of us could drive so I had to book two single rooms at their highest rate for bed and breakfast and he told the Receptionist to bung 15% on the entire bill for a tip!"

"The cheeky bugger!"

"Precisely! After all that, when I found him this morning troughing down porridge, full Scottish breakfast with haggis and tattie scones and half a loaf of artisanal bread with Dundee marmalade" – he paused for breath – "he had the nerve to tell me he had decided not to press charges anyway so that he could steal the glory for finding the room himself. As far as he is concerned you and Diana were never there. He has put the wardrobe back and will 'discover' the room in the Spring just in time for the re-opening of the House. He has a whole ad campaign planned 'the lost room of Sleeping Beauty' or some such."

I gave Jim his coffee and sat down a heap.

"What on earth is this going to cost me?"

Jim pulled out the bill and shoved it across the table. It made my eyes water.

"I think I would rather have gone to gaol!"

Jane pulled herself up from her chair.

"Give it here. Wow! It is on the steep side even for me but don't worry about it, Kate."

I snatched the bill back.

"You are not going to pay this Jane!"

"Too bloody right I'm not. Ian Bleakley is. I was hoping not to have to do this," she said tapping on her phone, "but he is taking the Mick here!"

"What are you going to say?"

"Well, don't get all sanctimonious on me Kate but I happen to have photos of a memorable evening his wife knows nothing about, let's leave it at that, shall we?" She pressed another button and wandered off to the privacy of the dining room.

"I'm going to bed." Jim moaned.

"Not until you have had these tablets, a shower, and a litre of orange juice mate!"

Jane came back into the kitchen.

"Sorted," she said, smiling to herself. "That was a fun night actually."

"I do not want to know."

"Please yourself. Now where were we before we were so rudely interrupted?" She consulted her flow-diagrams. "Ah, yes! This all came to light with the death of your secretary. Let's see that snuff movie again."

I reached for my phone and scrolled through.

"Here it is."

We both watched again as the Inverness express hurtled towards Berwick Station. There was Gillian standing alone on the edge of the platform. It looked as though she was arguing with someone, but there was nobody else there. As the train approached, she suddenly flew backwards as if some invisible force had pushed her really hard.

"Victim number 8 for Lydia I reckon. I don't know what she did to annoy the little bitch, maybe it was because she was leaving and depriving Lydia of a body to walk around in."

I had come around to Jane's conclusion that Lydia was the serial killer. What swung it for me was the character assessment of the priest at the time.

Count Beretsky had always struck me as a kind and trustworthy man, quiet and self-contained and sad at his marrow for the loss of his home and family.

"Jane, I think I know who threw Lydia into the River. Listen to this extract from Fr Birdsall's diary."

I set off immediately for Councillor Knox' home on the Quay Walls. As it happens, I ran into him just outside his house. I remonstrated with him in no uncertain terms. I pointed out that the Diocese would have paid the funeral expenses of the Count so that he could have a decent Catholic burial and that he had no right to deprive the Count of the Last Rites of his Faith and the religious burial he was due as a practicing Catholic.

Councillor Knox turned towards me with the look of a man who had stood at the very gates of Hell. It fairly shook me to see the difference in him. He had ever been a strutting little bantam of a man, but he stood before me truly a shadow of his former self. He then began a tale which more than explained the change in him and his actions towards the remains of the Count.

He took me into his confidence regarding a conversation he had had with his daughter, Lydia, aged 15 and also a pupil of Beretsky, in which she made certain allegations. I am sorely troubled by what Mr Knox has told me and yet I find it difficult to comprehend such behaviour towards a child.

"I think he found out that Lydia had not only made it all up and lied to him causing him to kill Beretsky but maybe also that she was the serial killer. It would explain the mysterious codicil to his confession."

"I was wrong. God forgive me. What I have done was for all our good even hers. God have mercy on us."

"If you put the name Lydia in place of 'hers', you see he is confessing to killing her for everyone's good. He had to stop her. Poor man must have realised she even killed her own mother, though I think he probably suspected that from the day it happened."

Jane's phone rang, I was praying that it was not another emergency that would whisk her away, not now. I was relieved to hear her say, "Hi Diana," then go on to tell her about the incident on the Old Quay Walls and the breakthrough we had made. "That was Madame Arcati; she is on her way, and she is bringing the Girls in the Band!"

Chapter 15

The 'Girls in the Band' stepped down onto Berwick Platform 2 from the last train from London at 11.30pm. There were never many arriving in Berwick at this time of night so few saw the visions who drifted along the platform in their fabulous fashions and fabulously expensive boots and shoes. Jane and I awaited their approach at the foot of the rail bridge.

"Jane?"

"Yes."

"Is that who I think it is?"

"Probably. You didn't think they looked like that naturally, did you?"

Gliding towards us were, and here I kid you not: four super models; two newsreaders; two actresses of the dame variety and two Hollywood 'A listers'.

"These people are coming to stay in my house in Berwick upon Tweed?"

"Yep. Well, they can't stay in a hotel, or the Press will get to know about it. We have to keep them under wraps."

"What do they eat? I don't have anything exotic."

"It's OK. Contrary to popular opinion, they eat whatever you give them. They are just people Kate, and they have all been through the student living on a tin of beans phase. They only act up because people expect it of them but among friends, they are just ordinary really."

As each of the visions approached, they hugged Jane with expressions of delight and shook me warmly by the hand. I was amazed by their beautiful teeth.

Jane had rented a mini-bus and they all piled in with their overnight bags. When we reached my place, the Americans were very complimentary and cooed over the age of the house and the original fitments. I showed them all to their rooms and not one moaned about having to share a room or that one or two had to use the bathroom at the end of the hall.

Diana had arrived earlier that day in her purple people carrier and while we were at the station, she had been down to the Indian Takeaway for their banquet for four times three. I had set up the dining table to its full extent and everyone tucked in, passing the tin takeaway trays up and down the table and chatting away like the old friends they clearly were. I had a lovely conversation about embroidery and gardening with the two dames then the A listers came with me to make coffee and load the dishwasher. They were all just pleasant people and good company. There was neither an air nor a grace to be seen.

By 2am, we were all changed into black leggings and long black tunics. Each woman wore the amulet of her own faith around her neck. I put on the crucifix I had since my Confirmation. Diana drove the minibus through the still, silent town and in minutes, we were parked on the Quay Walls outside the dreaded house.

Soundlessly, we mounted the steps. I produced the key I had retrieved from Jim earlier that day. Much to my amazement, it turned in the lock and the door swung open obligingly. There was a smell of damp, the chilly air of an uninhabited house but nothing out of the ordinary. Ordinary…not a word I ever thought I would associate with this place. Thirteen pairs of heels clicked across the black and white chequered tiles. Jane opened the dining room door and we all filed in.

Diana had brought a huge, heavy, black bag with her. From it, she produced two lead bars per person. She placed the bars in measured intervals around the great dining room table. Each woman picked up a chair from the pile of them near the door and sat with the iron bars in front of her. Jane pulled me to sit by her near the head of the table.

Diana then brought out white candles and white roses already in vases, bundles of sage and a huge bag of salt. These she placed on the mantelpiece and covered with a plastic bin bag. She approached the remaining chair at the top of the table on which she laid a long white wooden staff. She sat down and pulled a small silver bell from her tunic pocket.

"Are we ready, ladies?" she asked. The others nodded and I thought, *No!*

Then she began:

"Lords of the Eastern Watchtowers, Lords of Air, I summon and stir you up to guard the women of my Circle.

Lords of the Southern Watchtowers, Lords of Fire, I summon and stir you up to guard the women of my Circle.

Lords of the Western Watchtowers, Lords of Water, I summon and stir you up to guard the women of my Circle.

Lords of the Northern Watchtowers, Lords of Earth, I summon and stir you up to guard the women of my Circle.

Gaia, Holy Mother, Earth Goddess we claim your aid and protection this night that we may free your children from their earthly bonds. Give back to us we pray thee the spirits of those who have rightful business in this matter tonight that we may release them from durance that they continue their journey as is fit."

Diana turned to Jane and nodded. Jane immediately began her breathing thing then she banged her two iron bars upon the table and said, "Lydia Knox, daughter of this house, come forth. You are called to account and must answer." Then she banged her bars on the table again and so did everyone else.

No sooner had the sound of this knocking died away than I became aware of another distant sound. It was the awful sucking and splashing sound I had heard when Jane summoned her the last time. Sure enough, there followed the sound of her garments flapping as she struggled with her invisible assailant and the resounding bang of the outside door.

Suddenly, there she was struggling into the dining room, but it was when she stopped struggling that I felt sicker than I have ever felt in my life. She turned her whole body, smoothed her garments and stared with utter malice into my eyes.

"Stop that at once!" snapped Diana. "Lydia Knox, I bind you by air, by water, by earth, by fire. I bind you from North to South, from East to West, by sunlight, moonlight, starlight, twilight you will answer this night for your crimes and tell the truth before your accusers."

Lydia didn't seem to think much of this idea for she flew at Diana, floating in mid-air. Diana picked up her staff and pointed it at Lydia. She marked a semi-circle in the air and Lydia followed it until she slapped down in a heap in the middle of the dining table. Lydia lay there a pile of muslin, ribbons and curls apparently getting her breath back. The others at the table took it all like just another night in front of the telly.

Lydia stood up on the table and smoothed her dress and her ringlets. Calm, with a little dimpled smile on her cherry lips, she suddenly made a dive for Diana who lifted up her staff and knocked her to the other end of the table.

"You will get sick of this before I do, Lydia, I can assure you. Behave!"

Lydia fumed and foamed but remained still on all fours on the table.

Diana started her chanting again.

"All who have a grievance against this Lydia Knox here present come forth now and bear witness. Be you live or dead, within or without, above or below I summon you."

At that, the sash window which overlooked the river opened itself. A blizzard of snowflakes swirled into the room. They tossed and tumbled, whirled and wheeled then thickened into eight figures. They were not in black and white this time but in glorious technicolour. They looked for all the world like real people, not see-through or ghastly in any way. They were all smartly dressed and looked to be in excellent health. There were no gory traces of the grave.

Diana never turned to look at them. She just assumed they were there and called them forth each in turn to stand beside her. She began with Alice Cameron.

"Miss Alice Cameron come forward."

Alice stepped forward. She was a petite little thing with lovely strawberry blonde hair piled up at the back with little ringlets around her face, a budding beauty. She was wearing a pink dress with puff sleeves and a ribbon tied at the front below the bust. This must have been the party dress which caught fire and killed her.

"As you wish for peace and your soul's rest bear witness now against this Lydia Knox," continued Diana.

Alice gave a little bob curtsy to Diana and began, "Lydia came to my birthday party. I did not like Lydia, but Mama said that it would have been unkind and unlady-like to leave her out, so I invited her. I had a lovely day, and the best thing was when Count Beretsky played a waltz he had written just for me. It would have my name on it forever. I was so happy. When it was time for my guests to leave, I was standing next to Lydia in my bedroom and…" She glanced at the seething Lydia still on all fours on the table glaring and staring like a wild animal, waves of hatred pouring out of her. Alice's chin dropped and her voice faded away.

Diana sensed the fear in the hesitation.

"My dear, Lydia Knox cannot harm you in our presence nor will she after this night, please continue."

"Well…Lydia deliberately pushed me into the fire. In an instant I was ablaze. Victoria ran for help and the other girls tried to save me by beating at the flames. It was to no avail, but I love them for trying."

Diana turned to Lydia.

"What do you say to this accusation?"

Lydia laughed a simpering little giggle; she sat up straight and smoothed her dress.

"She was the prettiest. She had to go so that I could have the Count for myself. I am not sorry. It was obvious she had to go." She smiled her sickly cherry-lipped smile.

"Thank you, Miss Cameron. Pray return to your friends. Miss Georgina MacCreith, please step forward."

Alice stepped back as Georgina came forward. They hugged each other in passing. Georgina was a foot taller than the other girls and no beauty with a pale, flat face and mousy plaits wound on top of her head, but she had a capable air about her. She seemed like a no-nonsense, common-sense kind of a person. Dressed in a Saxe blue silk gown she stepped forward confidently and took her place beside Diana who said, "As you wish for peace and your soul's rest bear witness now against this Lydia Knox."

"Thank you, ma'am," said Georgina with an elegant curtsy, "Alice was correct in what she said. I was standing behind Lydia and I saw her push Alice towards the fire but with the horror of what happened and the sorrow of Alice's loss, it took me a while to realise what I had seen. I caught a chill at Alice's funeral and when I had almost recovered my Mama allowed visitors. The visitors brought flowers and chocolates. Had I known that the chocolates were from Lydia I would have thrown them on the fire. She knew I had seen her push Alice, so she poisoned me to death to save her own skin."

Diana looked at Lydia again.

"What do you say to this accusation?"

Lydia settled on one hip and looked bored.

"She was going to tell. She was always such a goody-goody. She didn't like me, and I hated her; she was so plain and boring. Nobody missed her I'm sure so why not? Mama had some oil of bitter almonds she used in a diluted way when we had coughs. I stole some of that then I removed the nut from the almond chocolate in the box and poured the bitter oil in. When I stuck the almond back on you could not see it had been tampered with and the clever part was it could have been eaten days after and nobody ever associated it with me." She giggled again; she was having a high old time.

Diana shook her head sadly.

"Thank you, Miss MacCreith, please return to your friends. It should now be the turn of Miss Isabella Watson and Miss Margaret Ross, but they have given testimony to us already which I will summarise for you now, Lydia."

The two timid ghosts had clung to each other throughout the proceedings. One in a blue gown and dark curls the other in a creamy muslin with rosebuds in her blonde hair. When Diana let them off accusing Lydia to her face, their relief was palpable. Clearly, Lydia had terrified them in death as in life.

"Isabella and Margaret had gone to the boathouse to speak privately because they suspected you, Lydia, of having killed their friends. You followed them beat their heads in with an oar and pushed them into the river to drown. What have you to say?"

Lydia rolled onto her tummy and waggled her satin-slippered feet, her head propped on her wrists.

"They were a pair of wet, brainless tattletales. They suspected me so they had to go."

Diana ignored her and plodded ever onward, giving each victim their day in court.

"The Honourable Victoria Paxman come forward."

Forward came the second tallest of the girls. She had large, brown, intelligent eyes and dark ringlets all over her pretty head. She had rosy cheeks and a cheerful smile. The material of her gown was far superior to that of her schoolmates, and she wore a delicate string of pearls around her throat. She walked as one who had practiced for years with a book on her head as she glided to Diana's side and dropped her a well-trained curtsy.

"As you wish for peace and your soul's rest, bear witness now against this Lydia Knox," said Diana.

"Thank you, ma'am. By the time Lydia came to see me, I was convinced that she was behind the deaths of my schoolfriends, but I had no proof. I had hoped never to see her again but, when she called, the servants showed her up to mama's morning room. I made it clear to her that she was not welcome and that I intended to ask my father to send me away to Bath to school so that I need never speak to her again in my life. She seemed to take this with good grace, and I was showing her to the door when she put her foot out to trip my feet and gave me a little shove disguised as an attempt to save me, so that I tumbled to my death."

Diana turned back to Lydia who was now sitting up twirling a ribbon on her ringlets.

"What do you say to this accusation?"

Lydia looked bewildered.

"This was entirely her own fault. We were just about the only girls left and because she had money and could introduce me in Society, I had every intention of letting her live. She was the one who was nasty and unreasonable, so I thought, 'why not'? She brought it on herself!"

Diana shook her head and dismissed Miss Paxman.

"Mrs Eliza Knox, come forward! As you wish for peace and your soul's rest, bear witness now against this Lydia Knox."

The ghost of Mrs Knox had been standing by her husband at the side of the group. She had a baby boy in her arms, wrapped warmly in a crocheted blanket. She was clearly reluctant or embarrassed or both but forward she came.

"Lydia told her father that the Count had behaved towards her in a vile manner. I blamed myself as I had left the Count alone with Lydia once or twice as I had to leave the room suddenly because of morning sickness. This is what I meant by allowing liberties, that I had left her alone with a man. Lydia told me that he had behaved disgracefully. I asked Lydia to speak to me about what had taken place and she suggested we talk on the Widow's Walk at the top of the house so that no servant might overhear. I agreed. When we reached the Walk Lydia began to scream at me, accusing me of having relations with the Count such that he was the father of my unborn child. I told her this was nonsense and tried to calm her down and as I went to embrace her, she pushed me over the low railing, and I fell to my death and the death of my unborn son."

I was struck by the calm way these spectres spoke of their deaths. I felt sure that in their place I would have leapt upon the table and knocked Lydia's teeth down her throat. They displayed little in the way of emotion as if none of it mattered anymore.

Lydia was avoiding everyone's eye while her mother spoke but suddenly burst out with venomous fury.

"She is lying the baby was the Count's! He was mine! He was mine! She had no right! I hate her! I hate her!"

She sprang up and flew towards her mother, but Diana once again blasted her to the other end of the table saying, "She cannot lie in this company, you silly little girl, any more than you can! She was innocent, she was your mother, she loved you and you killed her and your brother for no reason!

Keep quiet! I do not want to hear you! I will not call forth Mr Knox. He has answered for his sins at a higher court than this and been forgiven. Count Stanislav Beretsky come forward!" And forward he came.

He was tall and athletic of build. He was dressed in a military uniform; navy blue with a gold velvet collar and epaulettes, on his white stock a medal was pinned it was in the shape of a Maltese cross with a golden eagle falling from it. He had sandy blonde hair but in all other respects his miniature had not done him credit. He had kind eyes and would have had no trouble getting a gig advertising men's aftershave. Brad Pit eat your heart out. He smiled at me and gave a little bow.

"As you wish for peace and your soul's rest bear witness now against this Lydia Knox," continued Diana. He did.

"Miss Knox was enamoured of me I believe. I should have told her parents, but I thought the crush would wear off. It did not. I do not know what she told her father to make him have me killed and desecrate my body, but I can imagine, and I bear no ill will towards Mr Knox. As for Lydia, her rage against me was such that she would not let my spirit rest in peace. I had not the benefit of Christian burial. She exploited that and the power of her spirit, fuelled as it was by fury against her father and rejection by me after she had killed her rivals in order to get me, was too strong. She bound me to this house and when I tried to get help from people who visited here, she made me pay by attacking them. When I did succeed in getting out of this house, she soon found me and forced me back."

Lydia was now standing. She looked as pretty as any picture and was smiling devotedly at her beloved.

"How did you feel about Lydia? Could you have ever loved her?" asked Diana.

The Count shook his head.

"She was just a silly little girl. I thought she was a spoilt brat, and I would have refused to teach her, but money was tight. I never loved her that is a ridiculous idea. I felt sorry for her."

I think the worst thing one person can say to another in certain circumstances is that they pity them. Clearly Lydia agreed with me on this because as soon as the words left his lips she shot up to the ceiling and turned back into a hideous fish eaten corpse. She was obviously about to pounce when Diana said, "Ladies."

The Girls in the Band then placed their iron bars end-to-end and clearly from her various and furious attempts Lydia could not cross them. This did not stop her zooming from one end of the table to the other dragging her ragged dress and the smell of corruption with her. She screamed at such a pitch that every window in the house blew outwards and the roaring storm raged in, pulling at our hair and blinding us with stinging snow. She thrashed her arms and pointed her bony fingers at side tables and crockery in cabinets and threw them all at us with power and venom, screeching at us with foul curses all the while. The chandelier crashed onto the table, the doors were wrenched from their hinges and flung across the room, the very floorboards were groaning against the nails which held them.

"Enough!" cried Diana banging her staff upon the floor and to my amazement everything stopped. Diana then started a chant which they all took up.

"Judged you are and judged will be by God, by Allah, by Buddha, by Jehovah, by all the Hundred Names of God and the Holy Mother. Get you gone to the place of Judgement. Leave the homes of men and the graves of the Blessed. Be silent! Be Judged! Be Gone!" As they spoke, Lydia's shade thinned and the yelling of "No!" became a whisper and was gone. Even the storm stopped, and the snow fell gently now, minding its own business. Then the ghosts stepped back as if the whole thing had been choreographed and through the window came a rushing of wind, a whirl of snowflakes, feathers, wings and beings barely visible in the whirl of snow. They took Lydia firmly by each arm, she seemed to be screaming but there was no sound.

Much to my amazement, she was gone. Even more to my amazement, the other ghosts were all still there. The storm, the flung furniture, the chanting had left them unmoved. Diana turned to them.

"Thank you, my friends. Go rest in peace in the deep love of your God."

And they did. The Count helped each one to cross the shattered window frame through which they had entered and each one melted into the snowflakes just as they had come.

The girls in the band took this all in their stride as if they had seen it all before, they clearly had. They stood up and tucked their chairs neatly under the table. Diana set up a white candle and some white roses in each room of the house and gave me strict instructions to burn the roses once they were dead, mix them with salt and throw them into the river.

There was now not a single whole window in the house. I wondered about calling a glazing firm but decided to leave it to Jim to sort out with the insurance company next day. As we closed the great front door, Diana poured a thick line of salt across the doorway.

Before we had left my place, I had laid out a buffet of every Christmassy thing I could think of, to entertain the Americans more than anything. There were also sausage rolls, pizzas and quiches in the oven on a timer. Jane had filled my punch bowl with some lethal cocktail so when we got back there was nothing to do but dig in. Everyone stood around the festive board but despite my encouragement would not touch the food until Jane put a record on the player. I had heard it before, it was about limes and coconuts and clearly meant something to them as they all burst out laughing, sang along and dug in heartily.

Chapter 16

When I awoke next morning, they had all gone except for Jane.

"What time is it?" I yawned.

"11 o'clock."

"What!"

"Diana thought you could do with a good sleep, so she slipped you a little something."

"I never thanked anyone or said good-bye."

"Don't worry about it. They know. They loved the buffet by the way. Many compliments upon the quality of your Christmas cake."

The doorbell rang and Jim was there.

"Good morning, sleepy head. Finally re-joined the land of the living then. I have had a very busy morning thanks to you. I had a word with the insurance firm about the windows and they agree it would be cheaper to double-glaze the place than have it boarded and then replace the sash windows, so I rang a pal of mine and they have made a start on that. I think I can swing the carpets being cleaned and the redecoration of all the walls because of the ingress of snow. By the time I'm done, the old house will look like a new house and you can sell it for a fortune. Lovely views over the river and all the way to

Lindisfarne you know. In fact, a pal of mine is happy to offer you half a million as is including contents. What do you say?"

My head felt as if it had squirrels living in it.

"But does he know what took place there?"

"He's a developer, darling, he doesn't care. If it would make you feel better you can get your pal the priest to give it a once over with the bell, book and candle."

Jane poured us all a coffee.

"No need, been there, done that. There is not a single scrap of ghostly energy left in the place."

I drank my coffee.

"I don't want to benefit from Gillian's death."

Jim tutted.

"I think you are crazy but if you like you could sell the place and set up scholarships or give it all to charity."

That sounded like a good idea. Jane reassured me that all trace of Lydia was gone and that the house was fit to make some family a lovely home. At that point, the phone rang.

It was Wojtek.

"Kate! Where have you been? The funeral is today at 2pm. You will be there won't you? The Ambassador is coming and several members of the Count's family, including the current Count. It is a big affair with a Polish band and all the local Polish community and the Mayor and aldermen. Afterwards, there is a bit of a do at the Presbytery. You will be there?"

"Yes, of course I will be there, and I will bring a contribution to the buffet table, as it happens, I had a bit of a do last night myself and there are leftovers." It turned out I could also contribute the contents of a Fortnum and Mason hamper and a crate of seasonal booze thanks to the A-listers and the Dames who sent them as a thank you for putting them up for the night.

So it was that on a grey and gloomy afternoon in late December I was standing in Tweedmouth cemetery listening to a long funeral service in a language I did not understand when it happened again. I could have been sick all over my boots. It was the heavy hand of a man, the weight of long fingers, the pressure of fingertips. I turned and looked into the eyes of Count Stanislav Beretsky.

"Do not worry, Kate. It is not all beginning again. Lydia and all the others are gone. I am only here because I never received proper burial. I must speak quickly because Wojtek is about to read the comital. I just wanted to thank you for all you have done for all of us. I tried to protect the householders and visitors from Lydia, but her fury gave her such power I could only do so much. I could not save Gillian or her husband even though I did try. You were my best hope in centuries."

He looked so sad.

"None of it was your fault, Count Beretsky. You can go to your rest knowing you did all that you could, and no one can do more than that."

He smiled.

"Thank you, Kate. We made a great team, no?"

The mourners made the sign of the cross and Wojtek reached for the incense burner. The Count took my hand.

"Good-bye, Kate." He bent over my glove as if to kiss it, clipped his heels together and was gone forever.

I went to the buffet at the Presbytery. I handed round sandwiches and slices of Christmas cake, but my heart wasn't in it. After all that had happened, I felt a bit flat to say the least. Still, I only had two days before I flew to meet Tom in

Sydney. He was paying off his ship somewhere lovely for once and we were going to meet up with our daughter Sophia who was working out there. I was looking forward to a lovely family Christmas in the sun.

That night, Jim, Jane and I had our annual dinner at Manor Meadows. We always met up just before Christmas to exchange presents and go our separate ways for the holiday season. After a delicious meal it was time for the gifts. I had bought Jane a gold bracelet and a handbag by her favourite designer. I gave Jim leather gloves and a red cashmere scarf with matching hat. Jane pulled out a large box wrapped in Bugs Bunny Birthday paper. Jim seemed in on it, whatever it was, and they were both very keen for me to open it. I expected an explosion.

Of course, there was nothing in the box, just a Christmas card.

"I was going to wrap up loads of boxes of decreasing sizes, but I couldn't be arsed," said Jane. "Open the card then!"

The card was not a card. It was a first-class ticket to Australia.

"But, Jane, I already bought an economy ticket!"

"I know! I traded it in, and Jim and I bought you this. You can't go all that way cattle class. Anyway, we haven't seen our Goddaughter for ages so we thought we would come with you and there is no way I'm travelling second class darling!"

Jim poured more coffee and said, "Don't worry we are only staying for Christmas Day then we are going off in a campervan for a fortnight."

I could not believe it.

"Jane, you are roughing it, boiling a jumbuck in your billy can?"

"God no! It's a Winnebago and we are booked in to first class hotels all along the route. Should be fun."

They then started to argue about the route, who would be driving, what to wear, how to deal with snakes…I give it two days.

Next morning, I had to attend the Coroner's Court in Berwick and give testimony at the inquiry into Gillian's death. The police showed the short version of the snuff movie with Gillian apparently talking to herself and gave a verdict of suicide whilst the balance of her mind was disturbed. This seemed unfair to Gillian but who would have believed me had I tried to explain.

I went home, packed, took down the Christmas decorations, locked the door and jumped into the limo Jim had booked to take us all to the airport.

THE END